The Book of Hatma

By Atem

Translated by Dr Johan Janssen MD-PhD

CONTENTS

To Loes, Siri, Johan and Mickey

ACKNOWLEDGEMENTS

The manuscript was painstakingly typed up by Atem from the notes her husband made during their encounters with HATMA in 1955, so our gratitude goes in first instance to them, saving the story so we could tell it today.

It was the typing skills of Tracy Howard who made this possible in record time. We are in debt to Serena Waters who made a beautiful cover illustration. The cover was expertly designed by Emma Powell.

Lastly, my thanks go to my Editor and saviour in many ways, Karen Peradon-Alaga. Not only is she a fantastic, driven Editor with razor-sharp timelines, but she also manages to practice humour during times it all seems a bit much—so chapeau to her and Red Feather Publishing!

'The Book of HATMA' is for everyone, and we all should be grateful to Hatma for being given this manuscript.

Dr Johan Janssen, MD-PhD

Perth, Western Australia, February 2023

FOREWORD

I was introduced to the writing of Atem through her third husband. I first met him when he came into hospital and I, as the cardiologist on call, looked after him. He is an accomplished classical musician (flute, piano) but especially famous for his jazz, where he often combines classical themes, riffs, and classical structures/techniques, to produce a truly 'unique' jazz piece. Only the greats, like Chick Chorea, Keith Jarret, or Bill Evans can do the same. As an aspiring pianist, we made a deal: I would keep him alive, and he would teach me the piano, and how to play jazz. And thus, a deep friendship grew between us.

Atem died on October 23rd, 1993, at the age of 86. Although both Dutch, Atem met her future husband in Perth in 1955 and this led to a truly extraordinary future together. She was a concert pianist and composer, trained by the best in the Netherlands (Eduard Flipse and Willem Pijper, the best-known Dutch composer of the twentieth century).

"Her compositions were always a result of her experience of life at the time. She was a modest, unassuming, and extremely spiritual person. Paranormality has been described as 'beyond the range of normal experience or scientific explanation'. She firmly believed that she was guided to compose and write by an external force and that she was a medium through which beings from other dimensions were able to speak. Her belief in the existence of paranormality is an important factor to grasp if trying to understand and analyse her many compositions." Jeanell Carrigan

With Jeanell's permission we provide you with some sound files, accessible via QR codes which give you an idea of Atem's music.

1. The Reconstructed City

2. Lullaby

3. Pegasus Dance

4. Philosophical Futilities – Tomatoes

5. A Teeny, Weeny Little Birthday Symphony.

Atem's 'philosophical' writing started during her relationship with her third husband. Several books have been published, mostly in Dutch and several are available as e-books.[1234] The first one (unpublished till now) in this series is presented to you here: The Book of HATMA, typed up by Atem and her husband in 1955 and then translated from Dutch to English by me. I was able to interview him about this extraordinary experience and you can access the interview through the QR code.

Atem wrote in one of her works (Dhawana): "The impalpable, the invisible, the inaudible. For how long now have these been targets of disbelief, cynicism, and scepticism? Could it be that the impalpable, the invisible, the inaudible represent the real world, a world where the real criteria predominate?"

Enjoy reading 'The Book of HATMA' with an open mind, realising the era in which it was written (1955). In the afterword, I'll attempt to put this work in a (in my) contemporary timeframe.

Dr Johan Janssen, PhD

Perth, January 2023

---

1. The Book of Eron.
   https://www.amazon.com/Book-Jonathan-Eron-Books-Awakening-ebook/dp/B083PT2KS3

2. Het boek van de Eeuwigheid. Roma Hijneman 1996, Uitgeverij Kairos, Soest, ISBN 90 70338 467/cip (in Dutch)

3. Mijn Hemel, wat nu? Roma Hijneman 1975, Uitgeverij de Fontein bv, De Bilt, ISBN 90 261 3017 1 (in Dutch)

4. Het boek Godfried. Roma Hijneman 1975, Uitgeverij de Fontein bv, De Bilt ISBN 90 261 3021 x (in Dutch)

PROLOGUE

It is with joy that I comply with the request to write a prologue. It's my deepest wish that this book will be read, that the contents of it will be spread all around, that it shall penetrate to the deepest recesses of the human heart. Above all, I wish that it shall bring peace and happiness to all who will acquaint themselves with it. Why? Because it's the all-encompassing answer to the enormous, ever recurring question: what actually takes place after a human being leaves the Earth?

Much has been written about this. It has been discussed many times. Did not Jesus and many others do their utmost to explain it all? Everything that deals with this universal subject is basically very simple. Simplicity, so it is said, is the characterisation of reality. Only when one has gone through the entire range of difficulties and complications does one reach the point where everything reverts to perfection, to simplicity. And so it is with the following pages. Everything is open and clear, there is nothing hidden. When presented thus in a sincere and honest way neither sugar-coated nor weak, one can accept what is written as true and good. It's simply a continuation of the life one has led on Earth. And because it's a continuation, it's different for each and every one of us.

'The Book of Eron'[1] by Atem relates to the story of only one of many, many lives which are lived, but it supplies, I believe, an excellent image of the concepts which reign there, the different standards of life, the variety of surroundings in which life can be lived, and innumerable other things: but above all, the care and love one feels for one another.

Do I have to say more than that? It has already been too much, for the book speaks well enough for itself. Let me, in silence, pay homage to it.

Hatma

1.

https://www.amazon.com/Book-Jonathon-Eron-Books-Awakening-ebook/dp/B083PT2KS3

Music travels through the universe, continually cleaning and cleansing that what is no longer needed. And because of this, it can always be used ad infinitum.

Atem

1

HATMA, THE TEACHER

After the vibrant sounds of the previous words dissipated in the universe, we—my husband and myself—are taken without any formality to a place where we find a small, simple structure. It's made of a peculiar wood-like material, open on three sides with only one wall at the back, and with a roof which hangs freely. On the floor are mats and there is just one low long table.

We see the five figures who brought us here sitting quietly on the ground, dressed in white, legs crossed. They look like Hindus, Yogis or Buddhists. They quietly us that we must understand this has nothing to do with religious sects but are they are highly developed entities. They also explain that though we may think that one of this group could be the leader, it's not the case; they are all equal.

After this, we are introduced to one of the men and we're told his name is 'Hatma'. Our hands are put in his hands, and we're told he has been appointed to help and guide us, to work with us, and to answer all our questions. In other words, he is our teacher.

Hatma takes us to a corner at the front of the structure, and we sit down next to him. He shows us the beautiful landscape and the wide views. Then he notices that we're wondering what this big, gold-coloured terrain could be: is it grass growing there, is it corn or wheat, or are there flowers?

"No," he says, "it's the golden light that permeates everything and comes from the inner source of the earth itself."

We let this powerful influence work on us. After he tells us how happy he is to start this new task as our teacher, he takes us back to the other men dressed in white to spend some time together. And this is how our first and simple encounter with Hatma ends.

2

THE VALLEY OF THE LIGHT

During our second meeting, Hatma tells us he wants us to go straight to a different domain, an area which has never been seen by anybody from Earth. At the same time he asks us to leave our shoes behind because at a certain point, they would hinder us. He also emphasises that we must hold each other's hands for the entire trip, and we cannot lose grip for one second. We understand pretty quickly why he said all this because when we start our journey, we notice a loss of weight in ourselves. If Hatma hadn't held on to us, we would be in the same position as astronauts in their capsules when they float through space!

Luckily, this doesn't happen, and we walk at a good pace. 'A good pace' are not the right words because the speed we travel is indescribable. To lighten up the enormous empty spaces we travel through, we see tiny birds flying here and there, no bigger than two or three centimetres in diameter. They are beautifully coloured, and they play and flutter around so happily without any worries in a way we have never seen birds behave before. Hatma tells us they prefer to live here because they can express their enormous happiness here without any problem. And it also has a double meaning, as EVERYTHING has a double meaning in this unknown region. To every traveller who journeys through these regions, the birds give them a little piece of their happiness and their warmth.

After some time, we arrive at a terrain with all kinds of colours around us, above us, everywhere. They are magnificent and fascinating colours. It seems we're walking through a rainbow which has come alive. And as an answer to our questions, Hatma explains that it's necessary to traverse this colour field. We understand what he means because the colour rays seem to feed us with an unknown force, a force bigger than we have ever experienced. Hatma tells us we will definitely need this force sometime later when we're at the next place. We feel hesitant.

"Do we really have to walk over this?" we ask Hatma. "It looks very much like quicksand."

"Well, it's the reason we left our shoes behind," he answers us. "Anybody who has even the slightest piece of baggage will not be able to get over this field."

We understand that this, like so many other things, has a symbolic meaning. Because those who still carry loads are not free to cross the thresholds that lead to the areas where no baggage is permitted.

After we cross safely through this area, we arrive at our destination. We're in a big valley surrounded by high mountains. Although very impressive, this is not what piques our attention. What is really striking is the enormous strength of the light. It's so bright. And now we understand this is why we had to be reinforced by the rainbow rays in the colour field. Without that, we probably wouldn't have survived the strength of this light. After our initial amazement subsides, we look around us and when

Hatma notices we are wondering why we see humans, but no housing, he tells us, "You think there are no houses? Come with me and I'll show them to you."

He walks with us to the outskirts of the valley whilst explaining the following.

"A small group of men lives here in this valley. They only live here for a certain amount of time, just enough for them to fulfil a task. I could compare it to expeditions to the South or North Pole on Earth. Such an expedition is also time-bound because of the difficult circumstances in which they have to work, and that is the same here. After a specified time, these men must go back because of the strength of the light here. There is only one big difference between the polar expedition and these men. These men are not here to explore. These men are here to do a special job and the strength of the light is necessary to do that job. You'll soon find out," he concluded.

In the meantime, we have reached the foot of the mountains, and we can see that they've made living quarters in them.

"This is done," Hatma explains, "to allow the men to rest or work undisturbed. It would be impossible if the living quarters were to be placed directly in the light."

We're allowed to enter one of the houses, and we see it doesn't look like a grotto or an area carved out of the mountain at all. It's beautifully constructed, and the interior is luxurious, completely different from what we would expect. Hatma introduces us to the person who lives in this special house. He laughs when he sees the astonishment on our faces.

"Yeah, yeah, I know. I know how you don't like to hear from people who are no longer living on Earth. I know you automatically associate that with séances, moving tables with ghosts who visit, telling you stories about your dear ancestors. But you see, it's impossible not to recognize our host here," he laughs.

And indeed, who wouldn't recognize this man who on Earth had such a big influence on humanity? He's still dressed as he was on Earth in a white cloth. He is completely bald with large brown eyes that say so much, and his body is as lean and slim as it always was. It's impossible not to recognise him.

His working table is covered with papers, and he tells us that every paper is exactly one complete part of his work. And what does he do? Each day, he takes a piece of paper and goes to a selected place on the top of one of the mountains to fulfil the task. There is a different spot for each task. And from this spot he 'broadcasts' to the leaders of specific groups on Earth or other places. These are broadcasts of peace, understanding, friendship, and everything which is needed to improve our general wellbeing, though not for individual gain. This broadcast is only possible in this environment with the use of the most powerful forces of transmission. And that is exactly what these men do in the valley.

Oh, we do hope that the work of these good men leads to plentiful and effective results on Earth.

3

THE CENTRAL EYE

Today, as soon as Hatma presents himself, we feel he is very close to us. And he tells us we have to put our hands together again so that we're in unity, strong and unbreakable. This carries a lot of symbolism.

"This togetherness," he tells us, "is necessary and you will notice why this is the case yourself. Last time, I showed you a very special road that brought us to a very special place. There are lots of places I want to show you and we will do this, but all in good time. These roads are like rays of light that radiate from one central point, and it's this central point I want to talk about now."

We're wondering what this all means, but we sit down quietly and concentrate more so that we won't miss any points he mentions.

"As the sun is the central point in our planetary system, so we have, in a certain way here, our own system. This point is named the Central Eye. From there, the different rays are distributed. Everything is controlled by this eye and therefore it's also responsible for everything which is connected to these rays, which could also be called roads or ways. So, the special eye is ours and it has to be organised and controlled by us. This can only happen with close co-operation. Any individual who breaks or tries to break this bond between us will destroy the whole setup, and this is definitely not what we wish. For those," continues Hatma, "who are going the Way, bypassing religion, bypassing the cross, bypassing anything that obstructs the wider view even in the slightest, for those who are determined to reach their goal even when everything is against them, this is the first point to reach."

Here Hatma pauses and, for a brief moment, we have time to think about what he said. It's definitely something big, something that perhaps means more than we can comprehend at present, but it's also obvious that it's meant as a lesson. It may be a hard lesson—to push against culture and belief systems, but one then tests how far the elastic band of endurance can be stretched in order to reach the goal of the Central Eye. Now Hatma speaks again.

"I hear you asking questions and one of them is: is it really permitted to write all of this down? Definitely. I will never say something that is obscure or that should stay hidden. In this case, nobody can misuse our knowledge because there is one thing that keeps it safe, and that is we have an agreement, and the initiative is from our side. Because one day, we hope the time will arrive when everybody will understand these lessons in their full glory. When you reach the right point in your evolution, then you may be part of the agreement and, therefore take a larger part of the responsibility of life on your shoulders.

Yes, we've certainly received a lot of information today that we need to digest. And when we review the whole astonishing subject of the Central Eye, we feel that we'll learn even more than what is evident on the surface right now.

4

OUR SMALL ANIMALS

"Let's hurry up," Hatma says, "because there are festivities today and we can't join in if we're late."

So off we go as fast as we can until we reach a hard-surfaced road. It looks as if the road is made of one solid block of polished stone. At the end of this long road, we discover a door which is made of the same material and is as solid as the road. Hatma opens the door in a very peculiar way, by giving a certain sign.

As soon as we go through the door, we're in a sombre and depressing environment. But when we continue to walk, more light filters through and although still very unclear, we have the impression of a grotto which we subsequently leave. We enter another room shaped like a big round ball; a bronze-gold coloured sun. And when we are inside this sun, we see that there is something around us, something moving, although we cannot really determine what it is.

"These are gasses," says Hatma, "and I know what you're thinking now... that it might have the same effect on you as the rays the other day, but this is quite different as you will soon experience."

And indeed, these gasses seemingly have no influence on us at all, although it's a fascinating spectacle to see everything moving in and through each other. After we have walked through this closed environment for a while, we leave the ball opposite from where we entered. What a spectacle is now in front of our eyes! It's the happiest and most colourful scene we have ever seen. All kinds of people walking around dressed in multicoloured costumes. The women are in long, brightly coloured skirts, blouses with puffed-up sleeves, and hats decorated with fabric and flowers. The men are as joyfully dressed as the women.

"Yes," Hatma says as an answer to our unspoken questions. "I can imagine that you're comparing this with a festival from one of the Swiss Alps villages, but don't forget that we're not hampered here by countries, streets, cities, and so forth."

Of course, we believe him and then we mingle with the others. To our surprise, we are suddenly wearing the same colourful clothes as they are. In the middle of a square, we see a long but narrow table, beautifully decorated with flowers. Everybody takes a seat at the table, and we follow suit. However, there's no food presented, and we wonder what's going to happen. A man and a woman are seated on the short ends of the table. Obviously, they are the leaders of this group.

They ask us now to cross our arms and hold the hands of the people sitting opposite us. In this way, the table looks quite interesting, all arms and hands. Very soon, however, we feel an enormous electrical current going through us, and a tremendous feeling of happiness comes over us. We recognise this as the same element given us by the gold-bronze coloured ball, but even more so.

After quite some time, they allow us to let go of our hands, but look! Hundreds of golden sparks shoot from our hands. An overwhelming sense of great happiness grows in us, creating a deep feeling of connection.

Suddenly something else happens. A cloud covers us and closes us off from the environment, just for a second, and then everything comes back. They tell us that an outsider tried to come in but was prevented by a guard who was placed in the corridor by the door.

After the danger is gone, everything turns back to what it was. Again, we put our hands over the table crosswise and hold the hands of the person opposite us, and we feel the current running through us again. Then they place wooden bowls containing a crystal-clear fluid in front of us. They ask us to put our hands, still emitting sparks, around the bowl. Immediately there is a deep silence, though our bodies are still imbued with happiness. The suspense is enormous, and we can hardly wait to see what's going to happen. But we have to be patient, knowing that we'll find out in due course.

After some time, we see a movement in our bowl and this 'activity' is developing a contour, a form. While our excitement grows, we watch a strange event happening in the fluid. Around us, we hear exclamations of surprise and joy. Because here, right in front of our own eyes, a miniature animal is being created; more beautiful and cuter than we have ever seen. It's a kind of deer, although it doesn't look like any deer we know because it has a very long neck. We want to take it out of the bowl, but we're told not to do that and wait for another moment. Then the little creature opens its eyes, the most beautiful eyes one can imagine. Very carefully we take it out of the bowl, and we put it on its delicate feet on the table.

The creature radiates the purest happiness. We wonder if this is our very own creation, but whatever, we love this animal more than we can express. We then look around us and see that the others also have small animals, each one more magical than the other. What a happy carnival it is! They jump and dart all around the table and nobody can keep their eyes off them. It is through these little creatures that the purest and cleanest part of our hearts has surfaced, an experience that fills us with great warmth.

Now a large, unusual apparatus is brought to the table, and we're asked to sit and cross our hands again. Helpers remove all the little creatures from the table. The current is happening again, and the apparatus captures this new energy where it will be kept for later to be used to make new creatures.

After a while Hatma says, "Oh I'm very sorry, but we must go back now." And so we reluctantly say goodbye to our friends. During our journey back, Hatma explains to us that the original seed was already in the liquid of the bowl, but we brought it to life because of the energy created by our holding of hands. This explains why we didn't know which creature would evolve for us in the end. And so, another interesting day comes to an end.

5

THE THREE QUESTIONS

"I am not alone today. There is somebody who wants to talk to you regarding a certain issue. He wishes to put three questions to you. You can answer these questions the best you can, and this is all I have to say about it," Hatma says.

Just as we were wandering to where he was taking us and before we could think any further, he announces, "Here he is. Listen very carefully."

This is another strange kind of lesson. We have no idea what to expect. There's something mysterious here, and it gives us an uncomfortable feeling somehow. In any case, we'll soon find out what it is because the other person now speaks.

"How far is it," he asks, "from here until we reach our goal? This is a question that you cannot answer me now, but after we have spoken to each other, you will look at it differently. You know, when we begin to walk the Way we tread heavily, firmly on the floor. We're full of hope and determination. The road usually seems pretty straight and solid. However, after some time when we notice that the road is not as free of obstacles as we first thought, then our imagined unlimited powers falter, and several other factors shake our foundations. This is when our weak points are brought to light and tested.

"Many people, millions upon millions, take different roads to the goal. Sometimes they reach it, often they don't. Sometimes it goes fast and pretty easily, other times it demands what seems to be endless time, a period that brings them one difficulty after another. But that's not the point of our discussion today, and this is still not the answer to the question I posed to you. All the fighting, working, pushing, all the many ways to get to a certain goal, don't touch the crux of the matter. And this is why I'm here, to tell you this.

"I would like to start by making a metaphor. Just imagine an hourglass. An hourglass represents a certain amount of time, always exactly the same amount, no more, no less. One day it falls to the floor, the glass breaks, and the sand is strewn over the floor and blown away by the wind. Now there is no measure of time any more from the existence of the hourglass. Its function to measure time is gone and of no more use. And this is the same for each and every goal that we have in front of our eyes. We work and do our best to reach a certain goal and often we indeed reach that goal. But there may also be a time when the goal will disappear, blown away by the wind.

"Don't think I can't feel your thoughts. Who is this? You're asking yourself. What malice do you bring into our lives which are already hard? Please, wait a moment. I am not what you think. Let me get to the centre of this matter first and then I'll pose my questions to you. There is a deeper meaning to all this, a secret that can only be discovered after a long study with a strong will to dig into unknown sources. Wisdom comes out of the deepest part of the human being, and it's there we must search for answers.

Answers which are plentiful and are just waiting to be brought to the surface. Of course, now you want to ask that if everything falls to pieces someday, then what is the point of trying to reach that goal? Then there is no goal, also not in what I've just been saying. So why would we then put in any effort towards a so-called goal when in the end it just falls to pieces like sand in the hourglass?

"I know what you're thinking, you're right; this is where the greatest value is hidden. The wisdom comes when you realise everything is temporary and in eternal motion. That it's never enough to reach the goal that has been set in stone. When you realise this and still continue to strive for your goal, time and time again, then the amount of courage and power and strength one needs to do this shows, and it will be judged and recognised for its full value.

"And now for my three questions. See whether you can answer them, now you have all the information required:

1. How far is it from here to our goal?

2. Where can one find the answer to all questions?

3. What is the real truthful meaning of the world?"

After this, the voice is silent, and Hatma comes back to add a couple of last words.

"I understand very well," he says, "that all of this could upset you. Please understand that everything you hear or receive here is kind, beautiful and good. The subject of today was coloured a bit differently, but before we stop for today, I want you to understand that it's not meant to depress you. For the novice, it might still seem to be depressing, but for us, it reaches much further than the surface. And after some more thoughts from us, it's still indeed very good, pure, and beautiful."

6

THE EVENT OF THE PUFFING MOUNTAINS

"All of us—and today there are many—will celebrate an event that happened here a long, long time ago, and that is the story I'll tell you now," Hatma starts his treatise. "Once upon a time and they are still here, there were seven big mountains. They formed an enormous circle, a solid mass, and it was impossible to break through them. During this time, they released little puffs of smoke throughout the day. One small puff after the other. No, they were definitely not volcanos. They just were puffing; it did not lead to anything, and the smoke was not needed for anything in particular. All these puffs together made small clouds, but there were already more than enough clouds around and it wasn't necessary to have any more. So this is my story until now. Let's sit down here because I want to discuss this with you in more detail." Suddenly Hatma bursts out laughing. This surprises us, and Hatma sees this on our faces and laughs even more.

"Of course, you're asking yourself why I'm having so much fun," he says. "You know, really, there are two reasons. One is the expression on your faces and the other is because of these puffing mountains. I understand it's difficult for you to imagine what we're talking about. It's a crazy story, isn't it? Well, let me tell you, it's not really that crazy. In reality, it represents one of the rays of our central solar system, do you remember? And now we're celebrating this; the Event of the Puffing Mountains. It offers us the opportunity to come together and also to dive deeper into the subject. First of all, we'll investigate why these mountains make these unnecessary puff clouds. I think you've already guessed; for the simple reason to be important or look important. An importance that they really don't need because in themselves they are already imposing enough to be sufficient for the entire period of their existence. But notwithstanding that, they still want to exhibit this little bit extra which in the end, just makes them look ridiculous, and this is what we celebrate now—here together with lots of people. For starters, we're trying to discover where our own little puff clouds are hidden. When we find them and we're conscious of their presence, then we bring them out and tell the others all about it. This usually ends in hilarity and laughter, and in this way, we're all very happy to have had the opportunity to rid ourselves of these stupid little puff clouds. These celebrations are invaluable and while we need to put our puff, our pride, to the side, we deeply enjoy the end result—gaining a better understanding and appreciation of each other's deeper values."

7

VISITING THE CITY OF SOUNDS

"This will be a long journey today," Hatma says as soon as he sees us. "And I also want to warn you we'll travel with incredible speed so we can get there in the shortest possible time."

We're surprised, but we've learned by now to expect the unexpected and we follow him without saying a word.

After some time, we reach our destination and find ourselves on solid ground. Hatma always seems to have something new for us. We know that by now. The light around us is not very clear. It's dusky and we try carefully to find our way. But it turns out to be easier than we thought because the surface is completely flat. Not the slightest bump or hump and the terrain is not even hilly or full of scrub.

We walk for some time and then suddenly we come to a standstill in front of a large gate. It's solidly closed, there's no chance of getting through it. The light on the other side of the gate—and this is really phenomenal—is completely opposite to what it is on this side of the gate. It's an extremely pure, surprisingly clear white light, and takes a moment for our eyes to adjust. Although the gate on its own seems to be an insurmountable barrier, it's also heavily guarded. But Hatma gives a secret word and they let us in, placing our feet on a completely new terrain.

From all sides, we experience soft music. We realise that literally everything here emits a soft tone, and together it forms a kind of music, a music that's not curtailed by rules. It's completely new for even our trained ears. One guard from the entrance accompanies us and shows us the way. After some time, we hear a long tone coming towards us.

"Why don't you follow this tone?" the guard says. "When you deviate, you will notice the tone loses power and therefore it's easy to follow the right road." And with these words, he says goodbye and goes back to his post at the gate.

The further we go, the stronger this tone becomes, and then, in the distance, we see the contours of a large building. It sounds like this is where the tone is coming from and so we continue along our road with more certainty. When we get closer, we see that it's a glorious building. You could even compare it to a fairy-tale palace, standing there radiant and shiny in pure white light. And then, the moment we're close to the entrance, the guiding tone stops. Clearly, it's done its job.

Servants wait for us at the entrance and show us inside. We enter a beautiful large ballroom. This room has high ceilings and is decorated with gold and precious stones. Not a single item is dissonant, and we feel enveloped by a wonderful atmosphere. This is probably a result of the interesting sounds which float through the air. These sounds are not disturbing. As a matter of fact, they are soothing and fascinating to hear. Even more so than outside, every subject in this room is emitting a tone, and every separate tone is light and pure as a newborn dew drop. These tones are put together like a string of pearls, which together make sounds that we have never heard before, and we're amazed as we try to comprehend everything.

But then, after we have had ample time to absorb the wonder, we're asked to move to a little podium in the hallway. There we see seated in royal beauty a man and a woman. They ask us to come closer and again we feel as if we're in the middle of a fairy tale world. So we bow our knees and heads in awe of this beautiful pair, radiating happiness. And they give each of us a gift. An amazing, beautiful gift. A gift of rare quality. A gift that we will keep and cherish and guard until eternity because this gift consists of one single pure personal tone, and it's worth more than any other treasure.

Imagine for what purpose one could use this own personal tone. For instance, one can immediately recognize another soul tuned to the same wavelength as ours. One just has to listen and when the tone correlates with ours, we will be perfectly happy in the presence of this human. But there are also other possibilities for the appropriate use of our tone. There is, for instance, our tuning into the cosmos or any place we are in perfect harmony. But after these exciting experiences, we still have to return to Earth because first, we must fulfil several tasks in our life. In the meantime, we have the opportunity to think about what we've learned today and about the special gift that has been so generously bestowed upon us.

8

MEDITATION

"It's weird that we can see everything below us and nothing above. In other words, we can see what is behind us while that which is in front of us is invisible." With these words Hatma opens the meeting and we're waiting quietly on what will happen next. But nothing else comes. He just takes us to an enormously high mountain with a summit far above the clouds. Here we find a quiet spot to sit down and look down on the cloud formations. But we're not alone on the mountain. It turns out there is somebody else there as well.

"I often come here," he tells us, "because it's my task to bring joy to those who really need it, and this is where I prepare for that task."

Short and snappy, this is all we get out of him, but while we're here, we forget all the sorrows and problems existing at the foot of the mountain. Then with a single wordless movement Hatma asks us to use our time together in meditation. It turns out to be a very fruitful experience and that's why we have no regrets about this new way of travelling, and we appreciate the wisdom of our trustworthy leader.

9

THE QUESTION CENTRE

“Today I would like to ask you to concentrate your thoughts on an antenna. An antenna has to do with the receiving of broadcasts.”

“Yes,” is our answer, “but we thought that we on Earth are those who receive and not the other way around. How does that work?”

“Well, have patience and listen. In ‘The book of Eron’ one can read how a place called Glitter Town receives many messages. Not only are these from the inhabitants of Glitter Town themselves, but they also receive messages from Earth. It goes without saying that the messages are limited to the ones needed for Glitter Town itself. But now I’m going to take you to a receiver centre that works on a much larger scale.”

Soon we reach the spot Hatma wants to show us and we're not disappointed because it's something we've never seen before. There are massive, tall buildings all around us that look very similar to the ones on our Earth, like modern office buildings. We almost think we might be somewhere on Earth by mistake, though lacking in cars. We see many people moving from one building to the other, using a little floating square just big enough for one person on which they hold on to an upright pole for steering.

"You find it intriguing that there's no engine to be seen?" Hatma asks when he sees our expression of amazement.

"Yes," we say. "How can they move so freely and so easily without any sound?"

"The whole building complex is linked with magnetic roads," Hatma explains. "These are travel roads on which the small platforms can move. You could say it's the electrical power of the human that is steering the platform, putting it on a particular magnetic road, and working out where to go. Then the strong concentrated thought of the human moves the platform on the right roads to their destination. I also need to point out that in these buildings we have as many or maybe even more women working than men. Oh," he says, and then suddenly, with a quite different intonation in his voice, "I must stop my story now because I feel there are many questions deep in you guys. Questions that you have already pondered upon many times, and you really want to get some answers for them. You want a good and founded answer because, to put it politely, you are not taking it any longer! Well, this is the right moment for that. These buildings exist to answer your questions. It's very busy, you see that yourself. Let's enter one."

We're taken by surprise. What did Hatma want with us? Yes, of course, we have many questions going through our minds, as he rightly detected, but it's not at all clear what this has to do with these buildings. In the meantime, we enter one of the buildings into a vast hall with a very high ceiling. The entire area is covered in a pleasant clear light radiating from the essence of the building itself.

"More questions!" Hatma laughs. "Come, be patient."

There are long, shiny white tables throughout the building and indeed, there are mainly girls working here. Everything seems to be separated into sections and by each section there are boards on which a subject is written.

Hatma says, "So let me explain what all this means. This building specialises in everything in relation to… but wait a second, you have found out yourself!"

And yes, there in the middle of the building, floating in the air, we have found something. It's a big round coloured replica of the Earth, and so we understand that everything happening in this room and in this particular area has specifically to do with our Earth.

"In this big building, everything from Earth is being received, whatever there is to receive. Not everything that's communicated through radio and television and so forth because that is, in most cases, the least relevant. But this place focuses on anything to do with humans themselves. The number of subjects related to this is so incredibly large, that it would be far too much to dive deeper into it right now. In a nutshell, we receive all the problems the whole world is dealing with. Then the problems of separate nations, problems of separate organisations, of smaller groups, until we drill down to the problems of the single individual. Everything is recorded here, then sorted and is then sent to the right place to be dealt with. Believe me, it's much bigger than you think because the network is spread out for infinity. And now... give me your questions, because I can sense that 'you're not buying this'."

In the meantime, we reach a girl on which the board says 'questions about spiritual education'.

"We're in the right spot here!" Hatma says. "Alright, ask your questions. Yes, it's now that you have to open up and tell me."

We feel a little ashamed, standing here in front of this girl, but we can't change it and so we start asking questions.

"Well, this is all good and beautiful," we say, "but you ask the humans on Earth to believe in platforms that move over magnetic roads powered by the thought of the driver, and you want them to believe in buildings which in all probability also are constructed with the power of thought, buildings that emit light that is coming out of their own existence, of things that for us humans from Earth sound really fantastical and impossible. It's like a dream, a fairy-tale. How can we comprehend this? What do we have to do with this? How can you expect people to not only believe this but also try to understand it, try to study it, and grasp the deeper meaning of all this, of the unknown forces that are employed here?"

It's sad and so discouraging but also understandable that we're asking questions. The girl looks at us for a moment with a comical sigh and then pushes some buttons. Suddenly, in front of us on the table, there is a very clear-lighted cube. We wait in suspense for what's going to happen while Hatma looks at us with laughing eyes. In the cube, we see images pass by in three dimensions like in a film, but images that are still familiar and we can understand. It starts with events from the earliest period in the bible. Noah who listens to the command to build a ship, although he is being laughed at by his community and really doesn't understand it himself either. Moses who goes to the desert. Only God knows where he is going, but he listens to the order. And then further Abraham, who almost sacrifices his son because of the command. The prophecies and incredible acts Jesus Christ made. After that, many who suffered deeply because the world made a fool of them just because they fulfilled a task that they were told to do. Jules Verne, whose stories and predictions came to fulfilment one after the other, and in the end, they showed us the image of Albert Einstein and we're no longer asking.

The world we understand will have to go its own way until she reaches the point in time where all of this is not a problem anymore. We understand that knowledge will win over and the light will radiate over everything that is now still dark and not understood. Hatma sees our satisfied faces. With a thank you gesture, he says goodbye to the girl. We also thank her. Outside we look each other in the eyes and without further talking and with a much deeper understanding, we also say goodbye to Hatma.

10

THE NEW BUILDING

"Being together has a stimulating influence on us. Not only for ourselves but also in other ways," Hatma says. We realise this is true, but Hatma continues. "A group of my students is on holiday at present. Once in a while, we go on a trip to visit other places, to widen our horizons and improve our knowledge, whilst at the same time we relax. I'd like to tell you about a meeting I had with our students recently."

"This sounds a little contradictory," we interrupt him. "Everybody is on vacation and in the meantime, you say that you've had a meeting?"

Hatma smiles. "I believe I still have to explain it a bit better," he says.

We feel a little embarrassed. Why don't we have enough patience to wait and trust Hatma? But Hatma continues, not fussed.

"As a matter of fact, it's very easy. The task was that we would not come together in person this time because everybody was in a different place. But we still handle it in the same manner because we use thought."

Yes, now we understand, and we feel that maybe we're going to get a little bit more insight into the power of thought.

"As an important point," Hatma continues. "I would like to note that the outcome of such a thought-powered meeting could also result in a surprise for us because there are different combinations and different conditions every time. Therefore the outcome is always new and exciting.

"So, I was sitting there quietly, and I'll tell you what happened. I could feel the spiritual powers of the other participants bundle together around me. It was my turn to wait for what they decided to do. And it soon manifested itself. First, there was a mist that slowly thickened until, in the end, it melted into a cloud that completely surrounded me. After this, the cloud rotated and increased in speed whilst I was still at the central point. As soon as the substance reached the right speed, it took on the form of a disc and it began to develop in more detail. Now the time came for me to take action.

"I started by radiating life-giving powers to the new creation and, because of this, its mid-point lifted and rose higher and higher. Still higher it went, up and up, until in the end it was shaped like an enormous cone. Quietly, I remained seated, knowing that the growing process was in full swing. After some time, the cone must have reached its right height because slowly, oh so slowly, the top of the cone split open. From there, small, elegant branches came down. So many that it looked like a palm tree, except that the cone part was unchanged.

"Then, in a special way, I made the whole structure lift from the ground, carefully helping it to continue its development process. Slowly, it moved to another place, a place that it decided for itself, where it softly dropped back down. While the new creation was still open for further growth, I looked at it smiling, surprised, and in wonder. On all sides, there were windows and doors, all different in design. It was clear that every one of our faraway friends gave their own contribution, and although it definitely wasn't something that was made by an architect, the result was exceptionally original. For instance, one window was decorated with a porch while another was surrounded with flowers, and because of the great variation of this, it looked like the most interesting building you can imagine. The most important part, though, was this palm tree-like top, waving in the soft breeze. Not only did this give a very happy impression, but it also showed it was alive."

Here Hatma pauses. He notices our amazed look and then he laughs.

"I thought so," he says. "You're thinking it's a rather weird building and who would want to live in there? Well, I can tell you the answer to that very fast—my students have not only successfully completed the task I gave them, but also with good humour. One could say it was a student joke, an innocent one because I really enjoyed it. And who wants to live there? Well those that have a good feeling for humour, they're going to make it really special! But now I expect you to learn something from all this. If we are together in spirit, even the smallest task can be carried out if the intention is pure. Our new building is definitely an asset. It radiates happiness and joy and, as such, will serve as a living example of what can be established by goodwill, by cooperation of human effort, and by the very important aspect of humour.

11

MIND READING

"How far is the Earth from the sun? So far and still, it's so close. How far are we separated from each other? So far and still, we're so close. Distance is relative, therefore, in principle, you can decide this yourselves. And although it sometimes seems that we're infinitely far away from each other, deep inside we know that we're always very close together. And now for the subject of today," Hatma says and suddenly stops his lecture.

The three of us are seated in cosy chairs that are specially placed around a low round table. At the table we see a glass bowl which emits a soft smoke. This smoke is of a peculiar composition. It has nothing to do with cigar or cigarette smoke which, because of its bitterness, could have an unpleasant effect. This smoke has a completely opposite effect. It's permeating a soft, delicate aroma that, as soon as it touches us, has a cleansing and refreshing effect. We let this smoke work on us for a little while and then we see the result. It's as if everything becomes clearer; we can see each other better and feel each other's feelings better.

"Before we continue," Hatma says, "I have to explain something. The fact that we can all automatically hear and observe each other's deepest thoughts here in this realm is only partly true. We can keep those thoughts and feelings that are personal to ourselves, and I'll tell you why. A human covers most of his body with clothing so that he can keep his covered parts private. Although everybody knows what a human body looks like hidden underneath the clothes, we still respect their privacy, and that's the same with us when we're dealing with spiritual issues. Here, we don't show everything, and we respect this precious part of our personality that's different in each and every one of us. We can read general, daily thoughts and reflections, opinions, ideas and feelings of others.

However, the deepest, the most sophisticated and beautiful and, therefore, the greatest thoughts remain hidden from view. Now it can happen that a very close relation or a deep friendship brings forward the desire to get closer to each other's core and then we come together as we will experience right now. This glass bowl and the fragrances that it's emitting will help us forge a deeper, warmer, and more profound understanding of each other. It can also cause problems, but difficulties combined with a better understanding will still bring us closer together than superficial behaviour or small talk can do. When we know each other's deeper thoughts, this can then lead to an unbreakable bond with that person. Because of this bond, there is a powerful stream which not only keeps the bond alive but also takes care of its ongoing existence. You can understand that such a coming together can only be done when we know it's safe and can be done responsibly. I'm glad I was allowed to do this task today because it was not done from my own initiative. Maybe you can experience the same happiness as me and can carry the deeper knowledge that we are bonded by an invisible yet strong bond."

12

HUMOUR

"I feel very happy today," Hatma says. "By the way, everybody is having a lot of fun where I am now. Why don't you join us quickly so you can experience it for yourself?"

Hatma organises this and soon we're at our destination.

"What is the point of all of this?" we ask, confused, because not only do we see everybody here in the most fantastic, weird, colourful clothes, but we're also dressed in a fanciful way. We cannot deny it makes us happy too and we just let things happen, knowing that we'll find out later what the point of all this is. This place radiates happiness.

"I would like you to understand," Hatma says after we'd had some time to absorb it all, "that humour as well as seriousness is very important in the after-Earth existence. To be happy, to have humour in the best meaning of the word, is a gift of God that we definitely should not underestimate. If we didn't have humour—and how many people on Earth see humour as a kind of sacrilege? —then life here would also be unbearable sometimes. Since you arrived at this specialised area, you've already experienced the disappearance of sombre thoughts and worries. I have to add that we're not here primarily for ourselves. Of course, we love it, and we have so much fun which is obvious from the delight that radiates from everybody, but there is also something else happening here. Those who wish to give joy to others gather here once in a while to check in and catch up with each other. They want to see whether they have grown in the area of humour and whether they have developed to a higher level of education. It makes sense and is very pleasant to combine this growth with festivities. After this meeting, everybody feels regenerated, and this alone is a plus."

Hatma doesn't have to explain this because we also experience the uplifting influence of this place every second. To get to the bottom of the learning, Hatma continues.

"It's also a kind of schooling. It's part of the development which one cannot dismiss. Everybody who comes here has a task to think about something funny, something original. Some people think about this before they come here, others improvise on the spot. Of course, this depends on the personality of the person."

"Jokes?" we whisper timidly.

Hatma laughs with his belly, and says, "A thought you call a joke, and especially repetitive jokes, is the cheapest saviour for those who cannot think of something themselves. A joke is when something spontaneously bubbles up and is therefore a one-off. Everything is on a bigger scale here. One compares one's own capabilities of humour to that of everybody else. How sharp the line of thought is, how inventive they are in producing the kind of belly laughs that relax all tension. It's a fantastic stimulus for everyone who comes here. Don't think of it as a complicated task; everybody has an enormous amount of joy doing this in their own way."

Hatma now leads us to the spot where everybody can show off their humour in public.

"To get here, one must first go through a mill specially designed for this purpose."

Hatma explains the deeper meaning hidden in the symbol of the mill. "Going through the mill means that one has to travel a long road which is far from easy. A road where you must overcome all problems. From the sowing to the growing, the ripening, the harvest, the cleaning up of weeds, the milling, and in the end, its use as food for humanity. And it's the same with humour. Humour has to go a long way before it's ready to be used as good and nutritious food. It's our task to sharpen our humour so we're able to pass it on to those who are in need of humour."

We stay quite a long time in this place, and when it's time to go back to Earth, we're full of wonder and experience a deep feeling of joy.

13

SYMBOLS

There are four cardinal points: north, south, west, and east. When tied together by two straight lines, they form a cross. By connecting the four points of the cross, we get a rectangle. Because this rectangle is only resting on one point, it is also two triangles on top of each other. Because the lines cut the rectangle, it results again in four triangles. The cross itself is a plus sign and that is the reason it has a positive gesture. When we analyse this again, we see that the horizontal line also is the symbol of the minus sign. This minus sign under the plus sign means plus/minus, and with this, we introduce the element of chance. Again, looking at the starting point we will discover that the four cardinals represent the beginning and also the end.

14

FREEDOM, EQUALITY AND BROTHERHOOD

"At a certain point in our life, when we're in doubt about what we should do or which way we should go, then we really need help. Help is always there one way or another, but only when we're open to it."

When Hatma speaks these words, the atmosphere around us is impregnated with peace and quietness, and in this quietness, we wait for what will come next, whatever it might be.

"I will take you now," he says, "to a place which we don't really know anything about."

We only agree to go because we know—and this is something we have learned by going over the most difficult roads—that our instructors are 100% trustworthy. Off on another trip, we think. Yet another ray of the central solar system. Where will it take us now? But Hatma doesn't give us much time to think about it because he continues.

"I would like to simply go by foot today. It will do us good because we'll get some exercise. The road is straight, but we have no idea where it will take us. However, we must be prepared to follow the road and expect anything and everything. Let's go now and experience it for ourselves."

When he said this, one of us was feeling a bit dubious. Would this really lead to something? Would it be worth our while, or would it be better if we broke off the contact and forgot about it? At this moment, the other human presses the hand of his companion softly in positive support and we decide we will go further.

In front of us is a completely straight road, as Hatma said, and there's nothing in our way. There are no side roads and nobody else around. As we're walking, we're chatting amiably until after a short time we have to stop. There, right in front of us, the road is blocked by a wall of light, prohibiting us from going on. Light is so important in this place, we think. They use it in so many different ways. Many more than we ever could think of on Earth. At this moment, the wall of light opens up. Behind it, we find a narrow corridor which we're clearly expected to go through. This corridor is so small that Hatma has no other solution but for us to walk in single file. We look at him while he's thinking for a moment, then he says,

"You're wondering who should go first. Each one of us wants to let the other one have priority, however," and now he laughs as if he is up to something, "I will go first and thank you very much."

We have to laugh about it as well. We know by now that he has very good reasons for doing things the way he does. Like geese in a row, we go into the corridor, which we soon find is not very long. At the other end, we see a 'door closed by light' and Hatma now shows us why he had to be in the lead. We realise he must have expected the closed door. His hands make a symbolic sign, a sign that is too complicated for us to understand. When he does this, the door opens. We try to imagine what's behind the door and the wildest ideas go through our heads, but then, when we're standing in front of the open door, we halt in amazement. A wide-open infinite space lies in front of us.

"This is freedom," Hatma says. "Blessed is he who has this. No more roads with their many hindrances and side tracks, no obstacles, no tests that have to be fulfilled. This is the ultimate form of freedom, equality, and brotherhood."

15

THE CIRCULAR CITY

We're on a vast open field again, and we feel lost in this enormous space. No matter which way we look, we cannot see any ripple or obstacle on the surface. No trees, no bush, nothing interrupts this emptiness. Even Hatma is silent. When we find no obvious guidance; no means of a traffic sign or anything, we automatically think about the story that happened long, long ago when a star showed three kings the way. It was a star that brought them to their destination, so maybe we could also use this as a starting point. Maybe it's also possible here. So, we scan the sky to find a star. But we look too far because it dawns on us that the star is already here, deep inside ourselves.

We see a smile lighting up Hatma's face, and while he is still silent, we now know we're on the right track. After some time, we feel like the star is moving and, of course, we decide immediately to follow her. We look at Hatma for answers, but we don't get any help from him. It looks like he is treating us differently to see if we can work it out on our own. So we allow ourselves to be led by this inner star, which doesn't leave any doubt about which way to go. Slowly, we notice a subtle change in the atmosphere. Are we really seeing this correctly? The atmosphere is blue!

It is light blue all around and what an extraordinary phenomenon. Of course, blue sky is nothing special but to walk through a blue environment is very unusual. It permeates us, giving us a feeling of happiness. Our footsteps are lighter, and we continue along our road full of expectations.

'Road' is not really the right word because there are no boundaries or edges or anything that reminds us of a road. This would have made things very difficult if we didn't have our star, but now it's not a problem because she is pointing us to a certain area in a certain direction and when she does this, something amazing happens. Without being able to explain it, our inner star has a magnetic force because we feel her put us on a magnetic 'road'. The road moves beneath our feet, and we are taken along. It's lovely to glide so quietly in this beautiful, happy, blue atmosphere. There's still nothing to see, but this is perfect because now we can enjoy this extraordinary experience without interruption. It looks as if we can go on forever and ever but after some time, we see something substantial appearing in the distance.

The magnetic road smoothly brings us to a place which we can probably best call a city. The city looks like it's built in a circle and the first impression is one of cosiness. The word cosiness is used here purposely. We could have said beautiful or impressive or something like that, but that would give the emphasis on the outside beauty. And although it was indeed beautiful, the word cosiness explains the impression this city made on us. The same blue atmosphere is also present, but it's mingled with a beautiful radiating light that's not sharp to our eyes.

"Okay, I won't leave you in suspense any longer," Hatma says suddenly. We're amazed that he has broken his long silence so unexpectedly. We conclude that our inner star was working properly and passed the test since we'd arrived with no obstacles in our path.

"This is the city," he continues, "where many of our artists live. Those who stand the test of time, those who find pureness, those who went through streams and rapids, those who had to deal with many disappointments but still know from each other what they had to do to get here. Here, they create together. They grow because of each other's work. They open up for each other and know the responsibility they carry by living in this enormous circular city."

16

THE POWER OF LOVE

When we're next at the right place at the time to meet Hatma, he isn't there. Could this mean we can't continue our visit to the Circular City? This hasn't happened before and we're disappointed. We always think his presence goes without saying, and now we suddenly realise we cannot take him for granted. It hasn't even occurred to us the great privilege we have. So right there, we learn a good lesson and, in the future, will show more respect and gratitude.

But although Hatma himself does not appear for our meeting, there is somebody else to take his place this one time. Although we immediately know that it's not Hatma, we know this figure is waiting for us. We say 'figure' here. Why don't we describe him in clearer terms? Because we don't have any words to describe it. It's as if he is of a softness that you can't grasp, as if he is surrounded by a fog that you cannot penetrate. Why are we not going towards him or him coming to us? There is a certain distance between him and us and, as if by instinct, we let this distance occur.

Seated on a valuable-looking but still simple chair, this figure oozes calmness, peace, goodness and wisdom in a quantity we've never felt before. Still unsettled about this unexpected happening and not able to say a word, we're surrounded by a wonderful radiation which comes from this figure. We sit for a long time and many thoughts go through our heads, thoughts whereby we feel very small in the presence of somebody so almighty and perfect. We have far to go before we ourselves can aspire to be merely in the shadow of someone like this.

Then, feeling so lowly, the figure speaks to us. Though it's not a voice we hear, everything is clear, explicit and so obvious, nevertheless. We don't miss a single word. It's not like a voice inside our heads speaking to us. No, it's like soft veils gliding around us, veils which are made of very faint tender music of which each fraction encompasses a word, and as strange as it might sound, we completely understand every word. Each one penetrates very deep into the smallest corner of our soul. This is what the figure says to us:

"There is a force bigger than anything ever made by humans. A force which has never been measured, never examined, and never understood. A force that can penetrate deeper and further than anything else. Although everyone knows about this force, the force of love, she is not being used to the extent that she should be. This force of love is even greater than the antidote to evil and the expansion of goodness. There are several kinds of radiating powers: radiation of sound, of colour, tone, light, and it's the same with the radiation of love. This enormous power of love can materialise as sound, light, or colours and in this way, brought to reality.

"Now, we have to find the right concepts to explain what we mean here. When one meets Hatma and others like him, one may wonder what gives him this special presence. What is he giving out that makes people look up to him? It's the deep force of love that he has developed to the degree it's being transferred into matter, even to the point he can make his eyes appear as precious gems. Of course, there are no eyes of glass or stone, but we offer this metaphor to give you an idea. The surface of the eye is one big shiny, glittering orb with thousands of facets as if the sun made its rays shine from all the beautiful sides of the precious gemstone. This is a materialisation brought on only by the enormous power of love and this will touch the observer's soul, making them feel warm and happy."

At this point, the soft foggy sounds slowly float away, and we can't understand or hear anything else. At the same time, the figure softly fades away and for a long time, we sit as if touched by a miracle. We have been in the company of someone we could not even see or approach, someone who only came to us to tell us about Hatma's greatness and goodness, of the enormous love which he materialises into beauty. And now we understand what happened when we came to the circular town, where we couldn't find an explanation for it, because when Hatma stood in the middle of the city and he slowly looked around the whole circle, we saw that all the doors opened, and everyone came to him with joy to give him their best wishes.

17

THE COLOUR CHART

We're back in the Circular City again. It's a beautiful day, and difficult to explain the influence the blue atmosphere has on us. It brings peace and relaxation, and we believe it must be necessary because there needs to be a counterbalance in a city inhabited by only artists. After we've given the atmosphere a chance to work on us, Hatma says, "Now I think it's about time I tell you something about the people that live here because it needs a more thorough explanation."

We don't mind at all; we very much want to learn more about them. Artists are, after all, not normal everyday people.

"First, I have to tell you," Hatma says, "about the exceptional quality of their type of art. The general understanding is that an artist has certain expertise in one or perhaps a few different mediums of art, but here it's not like that. Every artist here can exercise every type of art. And now I'll tell you what this art comprises. You have, of course, music, drama, painting, sculpture, literature, dancing, ballet, design (about which we will discuss later), medical science, architecture, and science used to discover and invent things or improve creations. Then you have several other art forms as sub-sections of those previously mentioned, and then, in the end, we have the art of living."

"Oh, that's a lot!" we say, and we wonder how, first of all, everything can be present in one person and secondly, if it is, then how can you guarantee perfection?

"That's why they're brought together. Let me explain. The people who live here in the Circular City are carefully selected, as they all have the characteristics I just described. There is, however, one very important thing. Because everyone has their own personality, his or her colour chart is 'varied' as we call it here, and it's completely different from any other chart. If we imagine that certain colours represent each art form represented here, then how proficient one is in this art form dictates the grade of colour on his chart. Suppose he is busy with something and for one particular part of the artwork he doesn't have enough capacity to bring it to a good result, then he looks for somebody to help him who has that particular colour in abundance on their chart."

"So, will he then have to look at everybody to find the right chart? That's a lot of work."

"Oh no!" Hatma laughs. "It's very easy to find somebody because everybody has his or her colour chart on the front door of their house. It's his name tag, so to speak. Not only does it cut down the time to find somebody, but the owner is aware of which colours he needs to improve. In this way, it's very open and accessible and therefore an incentive for the owner to improve their deficits."

"This is quite a rigorous culture. Doesn't this impinge on their privacy and personal freedom?"

"Well, we're very fortunate here that we don't think like or live by Earthly understandings. Yes, on the surface, it might seem contradictory because one may assume an artist is often too proud to open himself up to critique, but not here. Don't forget what I said before. This is the city where all artists have conquered all kinds of difficult tests and only then are they finally allowed to live here. This is a much bigger task than you can ever imagine."

We look ashamed. We realise we still think in Earthly terms.

"First of all, the importance is the artwork itself," Hatma continues, "and it's very important to be perfect in all aspects. One of the biggest advantages is that they learn from what the other artist contributes to their work. That helps them to advance themselves in their work. The most important point is that through this cooperation one is feeding the art of living. By cultivating cooperation, the artists learn to overcome their baggage, like pride and egotism, to cast away their hang-ups and only advance their skills. It's so pleasing to see how many different artists worked on a finished artwork. It's all the more joyful than that of one singular artist. It's a common joy and because it's bundled together this joy has the greatest power."

18

A Demonstration in Design

Hatma takes us outside the city. It's a completely open and free space and makes us think about the open space we traversed just the other day, before we went to visit the Circular City. It's not completely parallel because here there is movement. Plenty of it. Everywhere in different places, one sees people working, sometimes alone and sometimes in groups, but all seem to be concentrating deeply on the work at hand.

"This big space is really the shed of Circular City," Hatma explains. "There is so much space here that nobody is in each other's way."

There are many advantages to not being bound by atmospheric problems, we think. Everybody can just work outside without any trouble. There is no cold, no burning sun, no chilling wind, and no rain.

"In the city, everybody has their own home. They can easily reach each other because everything is built in a circle. The round space in the middle is used for general assemblies."

Slowly, we understand everything a little better. In the meantime, Hatma takes us to a group of people; artists, both men and women. We can see on their faces that they've waited for us. They are very friendly and we're cordially received. It's clear that Hatma is not a stranger here. After a bit of chit-chat with the people from circular city—which for us is a very pleasant encounter as all of them seem to have a high degree of intelligence—Hatma comes to get us and invites us to sit on a couple of chairs that have been put there for us. They are beautiful chairs and very comfortable. They automatically enclose the body of the person sitting in them, and we understand they are the creation of one or more of the artists living in Circular City.

"We're now going to watch a demonstration in design," Hatma says, "and it's also an exercise for ourselves, so in this way it serves two purposes. The group of artists who are involved will now sit in front of us in a big circle while they hold each other's hands."

The other people present in the open space quietly continue with whatever they are busy with, although now and then, some come to see what's happening. These people were obviously just finishing their own work, we understand again, and we're amazed more and more that we seem to better understand what's happening here without getting an explanation first. We enjoy this and even feel a bit proud that we seem to have progressed. But now there's something happening that definitely needs explanation and therefore we concentrate one hundred percent on what Hatma tells us.

"Here we see how they work in combination," he starts. "To begin, we have an inspiration as the general basis. When this stream starts, you can use it as a vehicle to travel further. Really, it comes down to the personality who gives this inspiration substance to make it a reality. You, of course, know that this is a normal concept in design and almost all artists do this. Its universal influences being brought to reality. Right now, we just want to give a small demonstration of how design is practiced here, and we're very grateful that this group has spontaneously offered their cooperation. I notice you feel in the dark, but nobody knows what will happen. For this demonstration, we must determine what the starting point will be, and in this case, I have been asked to determine the subject. Our artists on the floor have made themselves very passive. The only method to receive what it's going to be is beamed to them directly."

Here he stops talking and we see him concentrate intensely for a moment. Fascinated, we watch expectantly, but no one can describe our amazement when we see the artists have instantly received the image Hatma sent them. It was so short and yet it seems to be all they need. They sit quietly in deep concentration.

Then we see on a spot not far from us, soft forms taking shape, faint at first, then slowly more recognisable. It looks like a painting but so real in all the little details. This landscape is created in the same place where just a second ago was complete emptiness. It's not a very large landscape, maybe six by nine metres, but it has the impression it's been there all the time in all its dimensional proportions. The painting is a tropical setting with palm trees and a kind of cubistic, almost Arabic building, very artistic in design. There are also some hills in the background and in the foreground, we see a kind of light-emitting sand that casts the whole scene in a very pleasant light.

"I have to emphasise," Hatma says, "that this is all their own creation as a result of the task I sent them. It wouldn't be at all satisfying for an artist if he could only make what was spoon-fed to him. But let's go to the next phase because, as you can see, they're now waiting for me to give them the next task. For the first one, I can tell you now, I gave them the idea of an Arabic landscape."

Again we see him concentrate for a moment, and then the artists look at each and laugh. What did Hatma do this time? It has to be something weird and yes, the artists, who now fully concentrate through tears of laughter, are busy making figures in the landscape artwork. No human figures, although they're still lively enough, but creations one sometimes sees in a cartoon or puppet show. As a finishing touch, all the figures are also dressed up in an Arabic way.

Everything is now finished, and they are waiting for a new task from Hatma. Then we hear music and, to our amazement, we discover that the landscape is being used as the set for a musical; a fantastic spectacle performed by the newly created characters. We can't but help to be mesmerised. It's so interesting and alive, so musical, with such fine content and form and with admiration, we appreciate the versatility of these artists. They must have had a long, long training to be able to make something so beautiful even purely as a demonstration for us. The other artists present in the area come to look, one by one and even men, women and children come from the city to watch the show. Everybody enjoys the offering, and we're all sad to see it end.

"Thanks," Hatma says with a warm voice at the end. We know this comment from him means more than any applause. The task was a big success.

19

MATHA (I)

"We have to move on," Hatma says, "because we can't stay in the Circular City forever."

It has been some time since Hatma's last lesson, but everything we've encountered so far is so fresh in our memory. In thought, we have thanked all the artists from this extraordinary city for what they showed us and what they taught us.

"This time we're going to move by means of our usual art of transportation," Hatma says. "I have to emphasise, though, that the different methods we have used so far are definitely not the exceptions because each and every one has a certain value, and they represent a certain goal as well. But we won't discuss that now. Let's concentrate on what's going to happen today."

"What do we have to do?" we ask Hatma, ready to agree, as ever.

"Well, we must 'want' to go to a certain place, which means we have to concentrate our thoughts so strongly that we automatically go there at the same speed as our thought can take us there. It's based on maintaining a pure inner body. Whenever there are different interfering thoughts, then the result is not as it should be, and we won't reach the place we want to go. Let's try together and see whether we can get the desired result. Is it perhaps a place you would like to go to?"

There is a place we would like to go, but we're unsure whether we should ask Hatma. We don't want to embarrass him with this suggestion, fearing it will be too personal. But Hatma looks at us with such shiny, clear eyes, it gives us the courage to ask.

"Hatma," we say with a hesitating voice, "where do you live, and would it not be possible for us to see it?"

At the same time, we see again the spark of enjoyment in his eyes we have seen so many times. Oh, we think, he is not angry about this question, but we're not quite sure because this twinkle in his eye is not there without reason.

"Do you know what's funny?" he said. "You have given yourself the answer without knowing it by the way you have put the question, and that is why I cannot help but laugh about it. You asked, 'Would it not be possible to see it?' It's a normal way of speaking but if you look at it closely it already includes a denial. Yes!" He laughs again, more to himself than to us. "Language can often lead to strange outcomes, sometimes mistakes. We need to do something about that."

That is all well and good, we think, confused, but it looks like our request has been denied.

"I'm sorry," Hatma says, although he still seems to gain pleasure from our grammatical faux pas, "but to do as you ask me is absolutely impossible. Certain things have their restrictions and the reason behind them is grounded in good reason. It's not the time or place to explain this in detail, but certain areas, certain spheres, are not accessible for people from Earth. Believe me, it's not possible."

Naturally, we take his word and get over the disappointment.

"I still don't want to leave it like this," Hatma says. "If you're happy to open yourself up, would you concentrate with me on the following; a desire to go to a place with me which I have chosen? We will get there as quickly as if we had all wanted it."

"Of course," we answer. And we drop into a moment of deep concentration. Suddenly we're in a completely different space. How is it possible? We're at the corner of a cornfield. What a beautiful view! Golden plump ears of corn in a field as far as the eye can see. What symbolism of prosperity, of completeness and utter richness, it's a joy to look at. In the distance, we see a woman in a light blue dress. She is picking and gathering some of the ears and when she has enough, she comes towards us. With a very friendly smile, so soft and inviting, she passes us the corn and at the same time she tries to make a humble retreat. But Hatma takes her by the hand.

"Can I please introduce you to her," he says with a voice as tender as we have ever heard. "Her name is Matha, and she is the one who stands by my side. The woman who is forever part of my deepest self as I am also a part of her deepest self. You have witnessed here a tender and pure thing and hope it deepens our connection for many occasions to come."

And to answer our gaze full of questions, he answers: "For the moment, we must be content with her quiet smile until the time comes when she can open up to others."

There is nothing to say. It's a testimony of such a great wisdom to only need a smile which in itself radiates such personality and gives us proof of our great friendship. We're so grateful for the trust Hatma has in us, a trust without boundaries. In silence, we let what happened here penetrate our minds.

20

A New Education

"We have been pretty active lately and visited several places," Hatma starts after we see him as usual and say hello. "In contrast to our last meeting, I would like to take you to a particular building. It looks similar to the one that we started in the first time, but this one is much bigger, and it's used for different purposes."

After a short while, we see what Hatma means. In front of us is a beautiful building, and in fact, one couldn't really call it a building. It has several marble pillars that support a big dome. The dome, which has all kinds of colours in it, is softly transparent and this means that the people under the dome are being sprinkled with a soft but cheerful light. There are several people there, men and women, but before we enter, Hatma says to us: "We're now starting a new phase of your learning. Every education has an endpoint somewhere, but one can always take on further education if they desire to. This new education will consist of classical talks, which differ from the hands-on experience you've had so far. Don't judge it straight away as boring or common or this will go downhill. Lectures not only require effort from the people who give them but also from the people who listen to them. We request the students put in the effort and if this happens, they don't need practical experience to learn it. Not everything we learn has a practical application."

While talking, Hatma has entered the space in front of us and we follow him self-consciously. It's clear to us that all the people here are students. Do we belong here? Aren't we terribly behind in the knowledge we have? We feel pretty ignorant. We're uncomfortable that Hatma put us in this situation without any warning. But once everybody wordlessly greets Hatma with respect and admiration, we are also warmly welcomed in their midst. We soon feel at ease as we sit on the floor like the others in big circles, one circle around the other. Hatma is in the middle, situated a little higher than the rest of us, and we feel that it's not because he thinks of himself at a higher level but simply because everyone can see and hear him better. When we observe more closely, we can also see that he sits on a moving platform so that he can turn in any direction. That is good, we think. It makes it more cosy, more relaxed, and because of the circles everybody feels included.

"This time," Hatma continues, "it will be only a short talk because it's our first get-together. We'll use the remaining time to meet each other, get to know each other better and exchange some thoughts.

"When one starts school in the first class, it's quick and easy to understand everything being taught. The further one goes in one's education, the more effort it will take. Once one has finally realised that in the human existence—and now I'm talking about both worldly and after-worldly existence—some things can be difficult and heavy to go through. But let it be a feeling of thankfulness and satisfaction because it's proof that one has graduated from the first class.

By the same token, we should not ask for more difficult times or challenges as the education will be hard enough. The challenges we face on the road are necessary, and it would not be wise to deliberately pile up more trouble. When one's education is finished, it's up to us to then go on to the next one. With all the knowledge we have gained in the former education, it makes it a joy to start the next one. One is prepared to tackle the new lessons and to know that every further teaching is met with an ever-greater clarity. I would like to emphasise that it's good to start a new education, especially when we know deep in ourselves that the previous one has been completed. When we study here together for some time, we acknowledge that we have all made this agreement that connects us; a continuous stream of energy floating through us. It's up to us to strengthen this bond. In this way, we are not separated but one. Everything of importance for one individual is also of importance for the other. When the one has to fight for something, the other one fights by his side. When one is happy the other one is happy as well. And out of this follows a multitude of forces where in other cases only one force would have been present. So remember that this relationship exists between all of us; that we're going this way together and will form a powerful and positive union."

Hatma asks us to get up and observe a moment of silence—how important silence is, we think. We all stand up together to meet each other and become better acquainted. We now approach people in a fresh way, knowing that we're now bonded with each other and have had the same level of education. Nobody hesitates to greet each other. Everybody is open and honest, and we sense that people feel as if they have known each other for a long time. It's a wonder that just a few simple words from Hatma can cause this, but we have learned by now that keeping it simple is the highest level of development.

21

REFLECTIONS

While we wait for the next lecture, Hatma has asked us to have an extra meeting with him and we're very happy to do that. It's always valuable to listen to his thoughts and, therefore, we're now opening our minds up to him again. Hatma suggests we join him for a short walk and so we pass through a laneway with high palm trees on either side. The temperature is perfect, tropical, but not too hot. The ground is bouncy, and this makes the walking very light. In the palm trees, we hear birds calling us regularly and laughing. We call back to them to say hello, which causes them to be even more enthusiastic. In the end, we stop calling the birds because we could go on until the end of time, but it makes us so happy. Hatma also looks happy, and we realise again how closely we've bonded with him. A moment later, Matha joins us. Now our company is complete, and we feel intensely satisfied. It's delicious walking like this, without any worries, so completely aware of the pure perfection of this moment. The greatness of the creation manifested in this environment reminds us of Earth, and we deeply feel that perfection can be experienced anywhere when one has the right mindset to make it so. Maybe that's the reason Hatma brought us here.

"The spirit is born, and thoughts can be put into reality," he says after a while. "The spirit is the greatest creation that has ever existed, and she will stay that way. This universal spirit lives in all of us and it works and grows, and through the working of this universal substance, all things are possible. In the ether, everything is present, and we can use anything we need from this pantry."

"How do we come to the right mindset for this?" we ask, because we feel many questions rise again. But even before we can get Hatma's answer, we see Matha's quiet smile touching us, and we understand that we're jumping the gun again.

"A child," Hatma continues, "already knows at a young age that there are many things he still needs. For a certain amount of time, he must go to school to learn about these things in a methodical way, and slowly but surely his understanding will grow. He'll discover possibilities hidden everywhere. Even when he finishes his education, he must still search further and work to get to the next phase of his understanding. One student will get there quicker than the other; it depends on many variables and circumstances. Still, the fact remains that everything is present, and everything can be done by using and applying the universal spirit. As you have experienced, I teach you these lessons to give you as much knowledge as possible, but you are not novices in education and so I leave a lot for you to find out yourself. Some things you have to work out like a puzzle, others you know you need to put the effort in to learn. The education you get from me is a free, self-determined education, and you know you can leave whenever you want to."

"This is not right, not *completely* right, Hatma," we interrupt him. "Because we're closely bonded with you and the breakage of this bond is not in question."

"Still, there is always free choice," Hatma replies, "and this one is meant to keep the door open, the door that gives you the possibilities to go back. However, I believe that in our case we don't have to worry about that and at this point we're all solid enough on our feet to keep our relationship going. The cooperation between us is much closer, much more intense, than that of a teacher to a pupil. My task is also to be a guide, as if I have been connected to you with ropes and I help you climb the mountain. And because there is a guide on the road, the time you need to travel the road, will be shorter. There are versions which you wouldn't know how to deal with that can be avoided when you have a guide, and when the guide is present you get straight to your goal. When you go by yourself you might lose your way or maybe you'll have an accident; anything could happen. And with this, I would like to close off our deliberations."

We continue to walk through this peaceful, beautiful environment for some more time and the highlight is when suddenly from another path crossing ours, we see a sweet little deer that goes straight to Matha and puts his soft nose in her hand. We feel we have witnessed the most perfect moment and to end our little promenade. We'll remember this for a long, long time after we have returned to Earth to fulfil our task.

22

THE PROTECTIVE RING

When we arrive a little early for our next meeting, it dawns on us that the company we're in is not as diverse as we first thought. Despite the fact that last time we spoke to several of the other students, something that previously hadn't sunk in now begs for our attention. Everybody is standing in a row, two-by-two, and we join them. But to our amazement, we see every couple is a man and a woman. It's clear that each man and woman belong to each other. And because we don't understand why this is, it must have a special meaning.

"Sure," a voice behind us says, and looking back, we see he is one of the fellow students with whom we had a conversation last time.

"Sure," he says again, "it's obvious there's a reason. Don't you know they give the education we get here to those couples who belong together? All the lessons are fully based on this principle. Single people may not find the same value in the lessons we do. For us, they are of tremendous value because they'll bring us further down the road we've chosen to travel together."

"Oh!" we say. We're taken aback because what do you answer to such a statement? In the meantime, we've entered the big domed space where we were before our lectures. In contrast to the last time, we see that instead of a circle, the people are forming a large triangle, facing what we understand to be the top point of the triangle. We place ourselves between the others and when everybody is ready, Hatma enters with Matha by his side and prepares himself for the lecture he's about to give. Matha sits down next to him and it's as if her soft personality creates a special atmosphere, giving us all a warm feeling of togetherness. Then, after a short silence, Hatma starts his lecture.

"Through extreme heat and hammering, steel is toughened. There are also metals that have a softer quality and therefore they exist for a shorter time. A well-melded steel is strong and indestructible and, in short, this is the subject of today's lecture. I would like to concentrate on the process of melting and forging this toughened steel, because not only has it come into existence by extreme heat and battering, but it's also a process of two or more parts melting together to become one. I'd like to start by taking a magnifying glass, an imaginary magnifying glass, of course, so that we can all see what others cannot. The substances we will observe are so fine and sensitive, yet they remain intact after going through a big or even bigger test than the steel we just discussed. These substances are not visible with a naked eye, and therefore, it's necessary to look at them under a magnifying glass and examine them further. What we're going to do now is concentrate on the substances of our soul. There is no instrument finely developed or precise enough to see how the substances of the soul are put together. In essence, the soul itself has to do most of the work and therefore every single one of them is separately heated and hammered, tested and again ripped apart, because when the moment of togetherness has finally arrived everything has to be precisely fitted. It has to be so equal in consistency that breaking it up is no longer possible. Now it's true that the two components (souls) cannot decide for themselves when the process is finished. One tends to believe that it now may be enough and we can melt them together, but it's only the initial creative body that can determine that. Only this One knows when the steel is strong enough to be united and this is what we envision happens in the triangle principle. We use this triangle principle because it's an indestructible necessity that will last for eternity. There's a lot more to this process than meets the eye. There are certain conditions that are necessary to make this union happen. Those who have helped the process keep a close eye right to the last minute.

"Next, I will give you a metaphor. When a world or planet is created by means of forging things together, and when, after a certain amount of evolution, it has finished, then something still needs to be added to keep it there for eternity. This eternity is safeguarded by giving it a protective layer or ring, which ensures that what has been put together will stay together. If storms or irregularities occur after the application of the ring, then this will most likely happen from within as it grows and develops itself. And the further the development happens; the less damage will be done. This protective ring is therefore proof that from the outside there is no way whatever has been created can be destroyed. This can only be undone because of problems from yourself, not from the outside thanks to the protection of the ring. So, you may continue your life knowing this protection is present. Here is a symbol for you to wear as a reminder: the golden, protective ring."

23

MATHA (II)

She is miraculous, and we have thought about her many times, especially this time. We can't stop thinking about her and when we see the puzzled looks on the faces of our fellow students, we know they're having the same problem.

MATHA.

This quiet woman radiates so much softness and friendship. Never have we heard her speak a single word. Still, it's as if we know her very well. As if we're very comfortable with her 'being'. Words aren't necessary to understand her. Somewhere, she has reached our inner selves and there is nothing else needed to attain a deep friendship. We don't want to give the impression she is still and silent like a stone

Sphinx. The presence of the Sphinx is shrouded in an air of secrecy. 'You want answers?' the colossus appears to say in mockery. 'Well, look to yourself for them. You won't get them from me!'

With Matha, we experience the opposite. We don't have the desire to ask her anything. What she radiates to us is immensely good. We would love to give her something back from our side, and one would never feel this standing in front of the Egyptian Sphinx. One could argue that the Sphinx is a great piece of soulless rock and Matha a warm, living human being, but her quiet essence has a different effect than the silence of the Sphinx.

In the meantime, we have joined the others and this time we sit in a long row, not inside but outside on the soft moss carpet in front of the lecture building. When everything is done and ready, we wait in silence for Hatma, but nothing happens. What is this, we think? It causes a little tension in us. We feel uneasy yet filled with a certain expectation. Will something special happen? Then it's almost unnoticeable at first, but slowly, stronger and stronger, we hear sounds coming toward us. We don't use the word 'music' specifically because it's more than that. Not louder, but more encompassing. Sounds that have their own being, almost their own personality in them. It's tremendously rich in content, very peculiar in composition, and it keeps us absolutely mesmerised. Our whole being is filled until nothing else is alive in us than these amazing sounds. We need to say that these sounds don't come through loudspeakers. It is simply in the air around us, and this is probably why we had to sit in the open air today.

After some time, the sounds fade away slowly and while that is happening, Hatma comes out of the building. Matha walks in front of him, carrying a shiny silk pillow in both her hands. There is something atop the pillow. The sounds are now barely audible in the background. Hatma and Matha walk along the row of waiting students, all in awe. At the beginning of the row, Matha kneels softly in front of the first two people. Without words, Hatma asks these two to give each other their hands. Matha puts the pillow in front of them and they both take one of the keys sitting on the pillow. The sounds are now gaining strength. Matha gets up and Hatma briefly touches both his hands on the heads of those who just received a key. When the sound diminishes again, the whole ceremony is repeated with the next couple, and so on, until in the end the whole row has their key.

Poor Matha we think, to kneel, get up, kneel, get up, what a tiring business! It would have been much easier if we all stood up and she could have walked past us to give out the keys. But interestingly enough, it looks like it didn't cause her any worries; she moves so lightly and so easily, almost hovering, it seems. We strongly sense this way has a symbolic meaning, although no word of explanation is given. This gesture of kneeling seems to be in a manner of respect and though we feel uncomfortable, none of us has the courage to protest. Had we done so, we would have destroyed the beautiful atmosphere created by the sounds. What a stroke of genius, we think. If we could have used words in this ceremony, we would have objected to the way they conducted it. Now we are powerless, and we see a smile of satisfaction in Hatma's eyes as if he challenges, "You just try and change it!"

We now sit with the keys in our hands, and it's not necessary for them to give any further explanation. We understand that this key was given to us because from now on, no doors will be opened for us—we can now open them ourselves. We will never misuse these keys. The sounds are in the air again, overwhelming and triumphant, and with that, this very special meeting is closed.

24

THE EMPTY CHEST

Today is difficult. It's difficult for us to get started. It's like we find ourselves too heavy to go en route as if we have an enormous burden on our shoulders and no power to move. We must get over this because it's time to join the others and be present at the next lecture. At last, our curiosity as to the subject of this lecture makes us get up and do something. Although our movements are laboured, we get to the place just in time. But the building we could usually walk in and out of freely is closed on all sides. It looks pretty though because the big round windows are sub-divided into smaller windows, each of them differently coloured. It surprises us when we see a wide, high door opening automatically when we come closer. We enter and resolve to leave all the questions behind us until it is explained. The others are already in the building, and we note the interesting effect of the coloured light playing over their faces. We feel a little bit guilty that we're so late and we hurry to the seats they kept free for us. This time we're sitting in a more classical fashion in rows behind each other and as soon as we're seated, Hatma and Matha appear on the platform in front of us. Hatma has something with him; it looks like a chest and Matha has a beautiful shawl around her shoulders in many striking colours which she shows us.

"Yes," Hatma says while he puts the chest on the floor. "Such a striking, colourful shawl is often a useful thing to have. Do you think we're playing a game? Well, you better wait a moment because there's still more to come." Our amazement is growing every second, and this is exactly what Hatma is aiming for; to have this excitement in us as if we're at a show where all our attention is on the person giving the performance.

"The shawl Matha wears," Hatma continues, "is like the light that falls through the coloured windows. It has a special meaning. We know how colours have certain characteristics, both on their own and when combined. Each characteristic has its own vibration that will fit whatever circumstance is needed, in just the right tone and balance. We should therefore appreciate the value of colours. When we are in spiritual need, we must learn to consciously use the colours to balance and restore us."

Again, Matha shows us the beautiful shawl she wears around her shoulders. She has an expression of joy and peace on her face. We also feel light and pleasant in this colourful environment. There is no more weight on our shoulders and our initial tiredness has gone.

Hatma now pays attention to the chest he brought. We wonder what's in it. Hatma laughs because his finely tuned receiver centre has sensed what his students are thinking.

"Yes," he says. "This chest. She is extremely strong, as you can see. You could say she is indestructible. She also has a double floor, not only as a secret space, but also to make her doubly strong so she can take any load. She is, at the moment, however, completely empty and if you lift her, you'll see that she is as light as a feather despite her sturdiness. I won't open her now to show you she's really empty, you have to trust me on that. Now, the important thing in showing you the chest is that it's our intention to keep her empty. Let's look at it as a kind of game, although it is serious, you must understand that. This chest serves as a vehicle to store anything difficult or heavy in our life. This chest can hold everything. As I said before, she is very strong and indestructible. But because of that, and indeed through that, the contents are then kept forever and ever. So now it's up to us to play the game where we must try to avoid putting our sorrows, difficulties and heavy loads in the chest. Otherwise, the chest will become heavier and heavier and heavier and heavier. In other words we have to try and get rid of them ourselves and not have them grow into an enormous load so that even this chest may not take it all in. Perhaps with the help of Matha's shawl or the coloured windows or the colours that you surround yourself with?"

25

FEAR

The walls erected around the building last time are gone. Instead, we discover couches everywhere, randomly placed throughout. It's clear we're supposed to lie on them. What a beautiful feeling to be so relaxed. As soon as you put yourself on one of those couches, it adapts to the contours of your body, giving the feeling of ultimate relaxation and quietness. When we've all taken our places, we hear Hatma's voice, though we can't see him. He doesn't seem to be present, and this surprises us. The voice is soft and clearly understandable, as if he is right by our ears. We see the other students are having the same experience. It's strange, but still it gives the impression as if one is being talked to personally.

"We'll now discuss a subject we have all, at one time in our life, had to deal with," Hatma continues. He gives a short introduction to put us at ease and to familiarise us with this newish way of lecturing.

"We're discussing the feeling of fear that can overcome us for one reason or another. Don't think we have not also felt fear. Fear can also stop us in our tracks or make us act in a wild and uncontrolled fashion. Fear of the unknown often makes people overthink, causing indecision. It can make things take longer to move forward, leading to other complications. Fear may also manifest in a more masculine way through denial, or disinterest, which may also result in pain or a difficult situation. This heroic behaviour does not lead them to the best outcome. Every medal has but two sides. Flipping it from one side to the other side doesn't help. We must find another solution. We can easily do this by saying 'Choose the middle road and you are always safe', but we don't necessarily like the middle road and it's for that reason we want to penetrate into what's hidden under the surface.

"Here we find an area of deeper thought, and I want to introduce you to that field. We can only enter this by using our conscious willpower. We need to draw on a strong power for this, a power that we must find ourselves. Nobody can help us with it. One cannot quickly attain this power because it has a deep background that has to be developed slowly through time and the different phases of life. We could compare it to a rapid stream because we go with the flow of it and finally arrive in a new world where everything has a different perspective. Where time is not that important anymore. Where distances are not of interest, and where a steady evolution can happen. This is the unknown where we can surrender ourselves to everything there. Where we can experience fear and peace side by side. A fear that doesn't imply danger for us. A fear that stimulates, a fear that brings us forward, where contrary images can merge into one. Where neither fear nor peace has a reason to exist but where both may be experienced in union for the perfection of their existence. This next step of diving into this deeper consciousness takes us to a place where we can accept fear, where our spirit develops to the point where we are part of the whole universe."

Here the voice ceases and there is only a deep silence. Not one of us moves. There is no discussion on the subject as sometimes happens. This lesson has been imparted deeply into each individual and each of us works it through personally in quiet contemplation. Soon we all dissolve into a peaceful, dreamless sleep.

26

BURNING

Today, something is happening outside the building. What a bustling and fun place! Everybody is very busy finding twigs and pieces of dead wood, adding it to a huge pile. We join in because it seems that everybody's doing it. It's really rather strange. We ask ourselves why we're doing this, but we don't find that uncertainty with the other students. In fact, they're laughing and not at all worried. Often, we hear them singing. We realise more and more that we, people from Mother Earth, are the most sombre of all the creatures here.

"Oh, what the heck!" somebody next to us says. "Everyone is free to do their own thing! Come on!" and with a laugh, they pull us into the group.

We forget all our worries and join the cheerful atmosphere. The mountain of twigs and wood is getting bigger and bigger, and although we don't have much time to think about it, we notice that all this dead wood, just as with us on Earth, is found underneath the trees. We surmise there must be a similar growth process here and so it would also have rubbish like the dead wood we're cleaning up now.

"A very good thought." We hear the same voice as before. This man, together with his female partner, has spoken to us many times and we like them very much.

"We're cleaning up here for a particular reason," he continues, "but we'll hear all about it later, so let's not worry about it now. Everything has its time and place."

The mountain of wood grows higher and higher, and Hatma and Matha are also there to help. Jokes are made left, right, and centre, and there's much laughter in the air. Then the mountain is high enough, and with a single movement of his hand, Hatma sets it on fire. Soon it's a bright fire, and it eagerly consumes the dead wood. After we watch it for some time, Hatma speaks.

"In this fire, we're now going to burn whatever we don't want in ourselves. Everything we want to throw away. Fire, after all, is pure and destroys in a very clean way."

Then he's silent. Is that all he has to say? What do we do with that? Hatma is giving us a very peculiar education indeed. But the others are obviously quicker to understand what he means because one of them begins—yes, we're hearing it right—he sings and whilst singing, he calls out what he wants to throw in the fire. In the background, the others all hum so we can still hear the first man's song. It's not a depressing song. No, on the contrary, his musical voice sounds warm and happy. He sings of the things he wants to get rid of forever, of his characteristics, things he has done. Symbolically, he throws everything in the all-consuming fire. As soon as he is finished and stops singing, everybody claps their hands in a rhythmic pattern. Then it's the turn of the next one. In the end, it's our turn and we're a little bit uneasy.

"No," Hatma says, laughing, "you can't bail out on this one, but we'll help you. Then it's not that bad. Try it!"

"Yes," we say, intimidated. "There is something we would very much like to get rid of, but nobody here has talked about this subject, so we don't know for sure whether it's appropriate."

We look around with a question on our face, but when we see Matha's friendly face, we dare to continue.

"Why don't you just sing it?" Hatma says, and yes, we had forgotten that we could sing rather than speak. In a moment, our song comes out all by itself and we have no trouble singing it at all.

"We want to be free of everything that has to do with illness forever!" we sing together, and we throw everything to do with this in the fire.

Then silence. Sudden silence. Why is it now so different compared to the others? Why is there no background humming? What did we do wrong? Are we stupid? What have we done now? It's always the same! Then soft and pure—is it a miracle we ask ourselves?—Matha starts to sing, and we all listen to her in silence. We're in awe. It's something that cannot be described so we won't try to put it in to words. After some time Hatma joins in with his warm voice, and sometime later, the others add a pleasant background sound. We feel as if their purifying power is a healing stream going through us, a stream that wants to have nothing to do with illness. A stream that is permeating us, that is taking over from us and makes us different beings—happy, healthy, strong. If we could take this healing back to Earth intact, it would be the greatest gift in the world for us. Still, we're not completely content with this thought. It's very selfish. Why should we alone have it when there are millions of people on Earth that would like to have the same? No, as long as we're people of flesh and blood, we need to be like our fellow human beings. But who knows, would there be a message given to us? Would the music heal us and also others? Does music have healing powers?

27

LABINO AND LABINA

On several occasions, we have spoken about some of our fellow students whom we have a very warm connection with. Whenever it was possible, we spoke to them or them with us and in this way, we now know quite a bit about them. We can't relate everything here and all the things we learned in the short time, but we thought it's still worthwhile to at least mention some of the things we discussed during our encounters. These two are called Labino and Labina and, like us, are not from this place. They must also make a voyage to attend Hatma's lectures and they also make their notes like we do. Let us state straight away that they're from a different planet. This planet is called LIMA, and it seems to be in a much further developmental stage than our own planet Earth. Our poor Earth will have to struggle a lot before it'll be on the same footing as LIMA. Whether attaining this is the aim of Earth is something still in question, of course. What struck us most is that they don't have any wars on LIMA. There is a protection system to deal with unexpected influences from outside, and this is predominantly in conjunction with the natural protective ring around the planet. The same protective ring Hatma discussed the other day, which is around nearly every planet. There was only ever one single invasion on LIMA and although at first it was surprising and frightening, it turned out to be a good invasion. They never had any trouble. On LIMA they are too busy doing other things than to quarrel and fight with each other.

The planet is managed by a group of extremely developed humans who are chosen because of their wisdom and the high degree of development they have in the arts. Maybe an example for us to follow! The planet LIMA has a particular interest in the subject of education. Our two friends made education their life mission and are very learned. Still, we were surprised by what they told us. For starters, the children grow much faster than on Earth. In their very first year, they go to school. A LIMA year is, by the way, different from our Earth year, but we couldn't figure out the exact difference. We got confused in our different counting systems. No wonder, given the short amount of time before we had to begin our classes. At this first school—let's call it primary school to make it easy—kids are educated predominantly in 'thinking'. To learn how to think in a good and pure way is of the utmost importance. No mathematics, no writing, but thinking in the right manner. They are taught to exclude anything of no importance which could only cause confusion. This results in selective thinking where the essence is kept and everything else is left out. Labina gave us a funny example. To give the smallest kids at school an initial lesson in thinking, she related a story called 'the grain of sand and the golden bird'. These two were having a conversation in which the golden bird repetitively corrected the grain of sand because she kept using the same word twice in a sentence. When the grain of sand did it again by using the word 'day' twice, the golden bird couldn't resist itself.

"You have already said that once!" he called out, insulting the grain of sand. "It is completely unnecessary to use this word again. It's a waste of time, a waste of space, especially when you are still so small. Maybe you should make your second thought 'night', for instance. That is the opposite of 'day' and that would then feed the first so that they keep each other in life, and you don't have to worry about it anymore. Learning, my friend, is a continuous progression!" and having said that, he strutted away.

After a year, the children have finished this primary school. The first year is predominantly dedicated to learning how to grasp the ability to concentrate. The next year is like high school. During this time, teaching and education are mostly practical. The kids go on road trips with their teachers and are taught many things on these trips. As a very interesting detail, we would like to tell you about how they interact with animals. Here the children have to use their own inner knowledge and apply it—'penetrate' Labina called this—to educate the animal step-by-step in the hard laws of evolution. However, it's not the time nor the place to discuss this further here. We also heard a very interesting story about how the children were taught the art of flying in the same way they're taught swimming on Earth. Then there is a kind of middle school, a phase that we don't have on Earth. This school is not a full year and so the students have a lot of time to do whatever they like. After this middle school, there is what Labina called the 'before last' phase because they call life itself the highest phase of education. We could compare the fourth schooling period with a university education. This consists of an intense training in all the different types of art, including a large portion of technical sciences which they also categorise under art. This education is so immersive that the students are obliged to live in dormitories and have no contact with the outer world during this period. Altogether, this education system is different from our system but in our opinion, it encompasses much more and achieves a much greater development education than the one we know.

28

THE WORD

Just when it really struck home how lucky and privileged we were to be allowed to follow Hatma's lectures, he announced to us all that we'd reached the end. This happened just before our next lecture, and we were quite shocked by it. Still, we saw the wisdom in it because we currently had no time to think deeply about what we learned. But it also meant saying goodbye to our fellow students with whom we learned so much.

Our last lectures had been unbelievable. We had so many thoughts going through our minds. Thoughts about the interesting and peculiar subjects that Hatma taught us in his usual unorthodox way and, without fail, had us contemplating long afterwards as we endeavoured to fully comprehend the message.

Now here we are, as we believe, together for the very last time, and before we walk into the building, we speak with our fellow students. We expect to see sad faces like ours. But to our amazement, wherever we look, there are only happy faces, excited faces. Hatma and Matha also walk around. Hatma talks to one and then another. We feel so stupid because they all experience it so differently than we do. It dawns on us that the others don't see this as an end but as a new beginning, and with this new knowledge, we soon feel better and in a much more pleasant mood. The sound of a gong calls us inside.

Like our first lecture, we now sit in a circle. Unlike the first time, Matha is present as well. She stands with Hatma on a platform, which rotates so slowly it's barely noticeable. Her soft gaze glides over all of us and we feel that this is, as ever, a very special experience.

"Before we start with our subject of today," Hatma says, "I would like to invite you all to a special gathering which we will have here at the usual time of our lectures. It will not be part of our teaching roster, but at this moment I cannot tell you anything more about this get-together."

He paused before continuing. "And now for the subject of today. It's one of the most important lectures in the whole series. It's about something that I can't give you as a lesson because it's something I can only point out to you. It has to come completely out of you. We have purposely done this in the last session because it's something that has to grow inside you. One could call it an end result. For those who are not far enough advanced, well then, it's simply not there. In this way, we can find out for ourselves if we've passed the course. It's a little like having a final exam. We don't have any exams, not written or oral. No, we're each our own examiners, and I'll explain how this will work.

"During this long time of working together, you will have noticed that perfection—the right, the pure, the truth—will always present itself without fail in 'simplicity'. Simplicity is the highest evolution because it has stripped away anything superfluous. Simplicity is reached by completing the circle that starts with the simple, the unknown, the not realised. As it is grown and understood, more details are added, and the matter becomes more complex. We may think this is the perfect end result, before we realize that it is overdone.

"Then comes the next step of sifting and peeling back until something incredible is left behind, finally the perfect end result. And now we will come full circle from all the lectures you have heard. You will find the perfect end result in the form of a WORD. This WORD will emerge from your subconscious to your conscious. Start searching deep inside yourself and when you are able to bring this WORD to life then that is proof the lectures have borne fruit. This WORD will be different for each one of you because of course not everyone is similar in evolution. I have to mention this, one WORD for every couple will mean the biggest success. This WORD will continue to play a very important role in your life. It is not part of the series of lectures that we have just done, but it will be used in a new period that you will all start very soon. The last task I will give you is to find this WORD. When you have found it, you will know with absolute certainty that it's the right one. And with this we say goodbye to each other until the next time when we will come together for the special meeting I mentioned earlier."

29

Intermezzo

It goes without saying that we took on Hatma's final task after the last meeting. It didn't work the first time, not the second nor even the third, but in the end, we did come to the right result. What a relief because you can imagine our unhappiness should we have failed. It turned out later that every other student in our group was also successful in finishing their study.

The WORD we reveal here is only ours and it has absolutely no value for anybody else because it's completely grown in and from ourselves. That is why it's easy for us to share our own WORD with you:
OMEGA

30

THE INITIATION

We're here again at our usual destination, and the building we're so accustomed to has had another metamorphic change. This time it's in the design of an imposing temple, artistically decorated in marble. It's a wonder of architecture. Inside, it's just as joyful to see. The light can only be described as pure. It's clear and so soft it makes us feel very quiet and peaceful. When we have taken everything in, we stand in anticipation in the vast silence. This time, the building isn't filled with music, and that alone gives the moment a larger meaning, because now there is only this all-encompassing silence.

Then Hatma is there.

We purposely use these words because he did not enter the usual way; he is just there, suddenly. We have never seen or experienced this before, and it takes our breath away. So radiant, so unworldly. Our teacher Hatma, our good friend. He has also dressed differently to how we have ever seen him. He wears a white robe loosely draped around him, held together with a golden belt. It looks like some kind of official uniform because he's usually simply dressed in white, as we described in the beginning. We're surprised because it's not in Hatma's style to be official. But even on this momentous occasion, we still see the little twinkle in his eyes, and then he speaks. (We wonder where Matha is, but we have no more time to think about it).

"Yes," Hatma says, "I am wearing an official outfit, but this has a very special meaning. On this last time together, I have also brought a robe for each of you. It's a robe so finely made and so feather-light that we don't even notice its weight when we hold it in our hands. When you receive it, you will see it's a barely noticeable soft blue. When you wear it, however, you will notice that it changes in colour.

A change that's completely dependent on your own spiritual state. Therefore, it'll also be clearly visible which grade of spiritual education and development you have reached. This is again another reason to continue improving yourself. Be proud you are on this road because it is very valuable. Always keep this robe in honour. It will never wear out because it's made from an everlasting material."

While Hatma is talking to us, we notice that an invisible hand has softly put the robe he describes around us, and although we don't see anybody, we feel and realise very well it was Matha who did this. How subtly this has been performed! Her soft, wordless aura is invisible yet still present.

Then Hatma continues, "We are here together in this temple because it is the symbol of everything concerned with the spirit. I would like to ask you all to come and stand straight in front of me and listen to my message. This message is a form of initiation to mark the end of the education you received here."

It's wonderful, we think, how so many things happen in a parallel way to our life on Earth. Today's ceremony is in a way similar to what we experience in our own schools, like the last evening of graduation. Now we're thinking about it, we surmise that these repetitive points of similarity are purposely designed. We have gained access to this unfamiliar higher realm for a short time and we will always return to Earth, so by bringing these familiar formats, we are able to acclimatise faster, feel more comfortable and perhaps absorb our lessons easier. In the meantime, we position ourselves in a row in front of Hatma and Matha, who appears holding a paper scroll. She hands this over to Hatma.

"The message I'm going to give you now is written on this scroll. I will read it slowly but only once and after that it will be stored in our archives from where I retrieved it. Listen carefully because it's important that you also keep this in your own archives, in other words, your memory. Don't be surprised about the style in which it's written because this message is incredibly old. Here it is:

'You man and you woman, you brother and sister, you daughter and son, the life which is without ending has taught you many lessons, lessons which were difficult and strict and became more difficult and stricter as time passed by. Lessons that caused wounds and of which you often thought impossible to surmount. But from this, you are risen and although you feel that your feet are still unsteady, it is as with a new birth. Your feet will get stronger, you will learn to walk, and you will take your place in the infinity of the immortal life. You will walk in happiness, and you will be a pillar for many. You will fulfil your task because you will do it with love, and you will be happy because you have conquered without hesitation. You have received the WORD in yourself, the WORD that is forever yours. Use it only in a good way and when you are in doubt, don't leave the safe hiding of your heart. You also received a robe that you are wearing now and that also will be yours forever. As a third, you will now receive the chain with the golden seal. This seal you will use to seal all documents you put your name under as a sign of sincerity and truth.'"

There is a short silence in which we let the words of Hatma sink in, deep in our inner selves. But while we are in this passive state, we see that the chain described by Hatma with the seal is invisibly put around our neck. Not by Matha this time, nor by Hatma. They are standing motionless on the podium with the paper scroll still in their hands.

"This has a symbolic meaning," Hatma continues. "There will be moments in your life when you'll find that something you expected to happen in the future has already been realised unnoticed. You will then feel and understand the value of the robe, the seal, and of the WORD. Let's now be silent for a moment and observe what will conclude this last session."

And while he speaks these words a ray of light, at first almost unnoticeable but growing in strength, penetrates the temple from above and covers us all in a pure clear glow. We are all part of it, including Hatma and Matha, and it is proof that this is not only happening to our small circle of students but that there is a higher power than Hatma which has had a hand in this. This beautiful sign makes us confident we can start the next phase of our existence and start it straight away.

31

HATMA'S SURPRISE

It's the time we would usually go to the place we received Hatma's lectures, but they're over. Finished. Forever. So what now? We're so used to this routine, and we don't know what to do with the emptiness that's replaced it. Oh yes, we know we shouldn't be saying this. Hatma has given us so much, so much which is forever ours. We know it's not right to push this aside and call it emptiness. Still, we have this feeling of desperation in us, and we don't know how to handle it. We feel far from perfect, though probably the contrary is true, and deep in us there is a strong desire to go further, so strong that we cannot sit still. We look at each other, look around our room with the many cosy colours, the plants, the flowers, our musical instruments. There's so much to do here, but again and again, the same thought creeps in. What now?

"That is very simple."

Suddenly, we hear a voice next to us. And what a surprise! Hatma is here with us in our own house like it's the most normal thing ever! And because it's a surprise, it's impossible for us to even utter one word.

"I came to get you," he continues. "Unfortunately, I cannot stay long in this Earth's atmosphere. It has something to do with the vibrations, you know, but I'm not going to explain that to you because that would take too long, and it would put my constitutional integrity too much out of kilter. So, come with me right now and don't forget to take your robe, the seal, and the WORD."

He doesn't have to ask twice and soon we have left the Earth's atmosphere and we're en route with Hatma at our side. Yes, now we're completely in our element! This funny feeling of emptiness has disappeared, probably because we're experiencing something new again.

"Of course," Hatma says while we're travelling. "I wouldn't be a good teacher if I just come with theories. It's the practice which is the important bit and that's something we're going to concentrate on today."

"Are the others also coming with us? Are we all going to the same place?" we ask.

"As you experienced during the first period we had together before you went to the common school, I have predominantly taught you both. The other students got into the school through a different route, received a different education, and had different teachers and lessons. They'll continue in the best way for them. It's all organised, and you don't have to worry about that. We now have a task to do. We're going to develop it together and hope we bring it to a good outcome."

Wonderful, we think. Anything is better than sitting idle. We wonder what it will be, but we don't even ask because we know it's pointless. First of all, Hatma wouldn't give an answer anyway, and secondly, we know that it will all be alright. Now we are content to leave our thoughts completely, we have the opportunity to look around us. We're gliding so beautifully and without any weight in an area which is light but still soft on the eye. We feel a warm fuzzy happiness and peace, and the joy of having Hatma with us is more than enough to give us a feeling of perfection. The atmosphere is so soft and so pure and to change the monotony of the environment we see, a small cloud glides past us once in a while.

"I am going to tell you something about that now," Hatma suddenly says. "We have enough time and to tell you the truth, it's also part of our plan. So let's have a better look at them. These clouds are of a peculiar and pure constitution. As you can see, none of them are exceptionally big, otherwise, we couldn't use them for the purpose we need them for."

"Need them for what?" we ask, laughing in disbelief. Hatma is also laughing.

"Don't look so surprised. You'll soon understand. Let's first start by choosing one of these clouds; one that attracts you the most. Then we'll discuss it further."

We don't understand a thing, but we still do as Hatma asks. We search between the clouds around us and suddenly there is one that draws our attention. It's as if this cloud moves to us, and the more we concentrate on it, the more she is rising above the others. And yes, we see her moving towards us. We don't let our eyes leave this cloud and this seems to stimulate her even further. Moving faster, she aims right at us until she is close by and hovers there, motionless. It cannot be more obvious and now we look at Hatma with a question mark on our faces.

"You've done that very well," he says. "Very well done!"

We're not conscious of having done anything special.

"Yes, you did. When the cloud and you both found a point of contact, you concentrated fully on it. This caused the cloud to react strongly and vibrate."

"Is this cloud a living entity, then?"

"Well, in a certain way, you could call it that. As you know, a cloud moves through space. Now you reply 'Yeah, but that's because she is being carried by the wind' and in fact this is true, but there is also something else. In essence, she started her existence out of a key concept, a principle that we all know. This key concept, this origin, is the true existence of the cloud and it's a living, vibrating thing. We'll delve deeper into the subject soon. For the moment, we must concentrate on travelling onward and focus together on the fact that the cloud is going to come with us."

So we do this and to our surprise, the cloud follows us. We don't have to go very far because soon we come into a big open space. We have seen this type of space before; wide, without any irregularity, empty and clean.

"Still it's not the same," Hatma picks up our thoughts. "This is from an even purer constitution and as you might remember the atmosphere of the last open space was blue. Here everything is white and even if you try your hardest you will not find one little spot, not even a single nuance in colour, because it's not allowed, as you will understand pretty soon."

There we are with the cloud quietly at some distance from us, waiting.

"What now?" we say again, yet this time our state is one of happy expectation rather than emptiness.

32

THE SECRET OF THE CLOUD

"The part of the human in contact with the spiritual causes a deeper understanding," Hatma says. "The human being who is open to spiritual development will pay more attention to something that will drift his way and try to catch his attention. He won't let it pass without having investigated whether or not it's of value to him. So let's now focus on this cloud. Before we do anything else, a better explanation of it will not go astray.

"Firstly, the clouds you've seen during the last part of our trip are not made from a common composition. Do you remember one of our lessons where we saw how you caused creation by strong concentration? We called it the 'new building' (chapter 10). I use this as an example because at the beginning of that exercise there was a formation of a cloud first caused by the concentration of all of us together. The cloud is what we manifest first when we're in the creative process. I'll explain this in more detail because it's of the utmost importance, as you will understand. The clouds like this are in one way or another spiritual children. In other words, they exist because of concentrated mind power, and they float around waiting for further development, further building of their young life. Let me add something to make it clearer. Thoughts always leave their lasting imprint, be it good or bad. That's why it's so important for all of humanity to improve and especially purify their thought life. I am not preaching, believe me, but it's a vital necessity," Hatma says passionately. He drops into silence. What must it mean for him to talk to us in such a manner?

"I am sorry I went too far," he says softly. "Excuse my human 'outburst'."

"You don't need to apologise," we answer. "We understand it so much better now and the whole point is that we understand it, isn't it? Preach or not preach."

We see him think about this and then move on.

"Now we come to the point where we look at how the cloud actually starts. There is a reason. It's not for nothing that you were so attached or attracted to this special cloud, and it's also no wonder why the cloud felt the same way about you. It would be easy for me to tell you why this is, but I'd like you to find it out for yourself."

For a moment, we're taken aback. Yes, we did notice that there was a kind of familiarity with this cloud, but we didn't have much chance to think about at the time. Now we do, and something forms in our brain. It's like the cloud is sending thoughts to us. Thoughts that remind us strongly—could it really be true, could it be them?—of Labino and Labina! We look to Hatma with a questioning face.

"Yes," he says. "This cloud was created because of the combined spiritual forces of Labino and Labina and, therefore, we'll now use it to work on further.

Pay attention. Is she not a beautiful form? Thin-aired and gracious, with an inner, never-ending movement. This movement is the very essence of the cloud. We could call it her personality. It's a part of herself that emits joy."

And look, as Hatma is formulating his thoughts, it's as if the cloud is coming alive, as if Hatma has brought his thoughts over to the cloud. A small flicker of light becomes visible in the centre of the cloud and slowly increases in strength. It develops more and more power and radiates towards us. Then, around this nucleus of light, something else is forming.

First, and it seems too fantastic to be true—it manifests itself as the materialisation of happiness! The light around the nucleus is the realisation of happiness and so protects the nucleus. With wide-open eyes, we look at it in disbelief. We're permeated with this happiness more and more. We look aside to Hatma and realise he is causing it. We really want to contribute and add our happiness to that of Hatma's. As we concentrate our thoughts, the influence on the cloud is immediately obvious. More and more parts of the cloud are now coming together, and these forms move towards the substantial matter being formed at the middle point. It slowly grows bigger and stronger until in the end all the different parts of the cloud are used, and the whole cloud is here in front of us as a completely materialised unit.

33

THE NEW WORLD

So this is it. Here we are practicing our knowledge and making it a reality. This is the real thing. We feel uncertain, afraid, not knowing what is happening, but we dispel this feeling quickly and concentrate on the cloud, which is just there, quietly waiting. With a calm and unforced attention, we begin. We keep the path clear of thought to enhance the concentration on our intention. Something deep inside is expanded and we forget our own existence. We focus fully on this one point, pure, strong, but full of love. Because this last piece—love—has been added to it, and it's like a revelation. Like a rosebud growing and opening up in spring. The bud doesn't consciously decide to open but unfurls when the time is right.

Our soft breath comes over our lips regularly with control. Not in the least related to a feeling of excitement. It glides forth, unnoticed and changes into the letter O. The first letter of our WORD! It's so liberating to hear this tender, pure tone, and as its purity increases in force then our happiness is unbelievable, and we can say with no hesitation we're in an elevated state. The WORD is a long, smooth and clear road, growing to a completeness, but it's not enough. Again and again we repeat it. Singing in its full glory and commitment, stronger and more powerful every time. Elevated in tone, elevated until it has reached the greatest height and look, it's as if there is a miracle happening.

More parts are being added to our cloud. First, almost invisibly fine and transparent, but getting denser and thicker. These parts accelerate and it looks as if they can't turn around quick enough because they are intent on bringing the WORD to life. They jump all over each other, flowing everywhere, coloured with different nuances, and they put themselves together. We sense the great pleasure they have in doing this job. They are building, working like busy bees being carried on the roads of sound. They build further and further and the whole thing takes more shape. First, we think it will take one form, then a different one, but in its unstoppable movement, it's impossible to yet define.

We have lost all sense of time and have no idea how long it's taken. It has to be a long time though, because when we slowly come back to ourselves, our powers are waning and we understand that the tempo needs to slow down. Our voices sing more softly, though the tone still keeps its height. But in the end, it's all over, and although the cloud is still moving, she seems to have reached the end phase.

It's fascinating to watch. It this real? Is this our work? It's almost unbelievable. We have created a sphere, floating in a circular fashion. It's not as big, but it's a kind of Earth. We weep, but then Hatma comes to the rescue. He also seems to be moved because he grabs our hands without saying a word. In this way, all three of us stand and gaze at the miracle. The light centre is still faintly visible inside the sphere. It's a good planet. A good and pure world. Nothing has been defiled.

Oh, how we hope it will stay like this. Is this reality? Is this our work? Then Hatma speaks.

"Don't think that this is a symbolic world and therefore she might just disappear in smoke. No, it will take a place in the wider universe. It will take a long time for it to grow and develop. It will take a long time before she has reached the stage where she'll be useful. You'll know something about that in the future, but we're not going to gallop ahead of ourselves. Her name? Of course you gave it to her yourself. 'OMEGA'."

Then Hatma stops talking and we're also silent because what is there to say? We feel so small, and not a word can come from our lips. The ball rotates softly. We don't realise at first, but it's clear that it's distancing itself from us slowly but surely. She goes further away, and then we understand she's going to take her place in the big universe. Our thoughts and best wishes go with her; this new creation which is purely there because of the culmination of our forces. The forces of those who are bonded and only want the best and the purest for their creation.

Bon chance OMEGA! Lots of luck!

34

THE SQUARE HOUSE

When the sphere has disappeared into the distance, we understand that there's no point in staying in the same spot any longer. Hatma confirms our thoughts when he appears again at our usual time to educate us further.

"So where to now?" we ask, while feeling a little timid.

"A very natural question," Hatma replies. "But don't forget, we are now practicing everything you learned in daily life as much as possible. Try to remember. What do you think I mean?"

"Ah! The star!" we shout out in one voice. "We almost forgot about that. It's still alive deep inside us, and we just have to follow it to reach our next destination."

Hatma, of course, knows the destination, but now he leaves everything up to us. We wonder how difficult this practical part of our education will be. We think we'll have to try very hard to do the best we can. And then we remember that simplicity must also be applied, so the idea of 'effort' must be crossed off the list.

"Can't you help us a little bit?" we ask Hatma. "It's all so new and we're finding it pretty difficult."

Hatma laughs. "You have already forgotten there are certain magnetic roads that bring us to where we want to be in a straight line. When you navigate by means of your inner star—in other words, your instinct—you'll find this helps your cause considerably."

This is a really important pointer, and we use it straight away. And yes, when we find the right direction with confidence, we feel we're on the right road. Faster than the thought, we're moving forwards, and in the shortest possible time, we land in the place that we assume must be our destination. It's a wonder, we think! We really didn't know where we were meant to go and still our own inner self brought us here. Well, to be completely honest, guided by Hatma, of course. We can never forget that!

We put our attention on what we find. It's not very busy and there aren't many buildings. It's simplicity in the extreme but as we now know, this is more often an advantage than a disadvantage, so we don't worry about it. There is only one building and we don't see any living creatures. The building is an enormous house and completely square. We can't see any windows or doors, so it looks inaccessible from the outside. There's a beautiful garden around the house, with a different design and planting on each of the four sides, and this softens the imposing impression of the building. How do we get inside here, and must we again solve that problem ourselves?

"Do you want to go inside?" Hatma asks. "Although 'want to' is not enough in this case. You must also desire to be welcomed in this house, otherwise you won't get in with by just 'wanting to'."

We follow Hatma's advice and yes, after a short while, something is happening. A kind of platform is lowered down in front of us. We get on and it rises. Softly, it hovers over the house and then it lowers itself gently into a courtyard in the middle of the building. We can't hide our amazement. "We have travelled a long way to this place. Couldn't we also do this last bit ourselves?" we ask.

"You forget that I explained you must be welcome here," Hatma replies. "This building is hermetically closed from the outside so that even with the best 'will', you cannot get in without being invited."

Now we understand it better and we look around. At the moment, we can't see anyone else, but we have our suspicions. We need to pay attention to the building from this inner courtyard. We never would have expected something like this within the walls of an uninviting building. There is nothing of the straight lines that amazed us from the outside. But inside we feel we're in an oasis.

The courtyard, of course, is square and has a pond in the middle containing many coloured fish. But wait a second, what's this? These fish also seem to be comfortable outside the water because several are on the grass around the pond. They play with each other and make the most wonderful sounds. Sometimes they slide back into the water where they have all kinds of toys and amuse themselves. They jump in and out and it's a joy to behold.

Beyond the grass, the ground is white to the edge of the galleries running along the four sides of the building. Every surface of the galleries is covered with a kind of living natural material that seems to be somewhere in between grass and plants. It looks like grass, but then we see flowers everywhere in between. The light in these galleries is very soothing. It would be wonderful to sit here.

Then Hatma asks us to follow him, and he brings us to a large arched door in one of the four sides. As we approach, the door is opened from inside; by Matha—we're so happy to see her!

"Here you are finally!"

This gives us more joy than we can say. She warmly welcomes us to come inside and we're happy to accept. The space inside is enormous. It's the complete area of one of the four sides of the building. The interior is stylish with a warm cosiness. Could it be any way different with Matha in charge? There's not a lot of furniture, but it seems very comfortable. Our attention is drawn to beautiful works of art. What an interior to stay in! When we let everything sink in, Hatma invites us to take a chair. Matha sits on a silk pillow on the floor, and we sit on chairs that form to our body shape. Hatma brings us a refreshing drink. We drink it in silence because the mood is too good to spoil by speaking. But then Hatma explains.

"This building," he says, "is used for conferences. Not any type of conference, but for conferences that take a longer time and also discuss a particular subject. We'll keep the subject a secret for the moment. One couple resides in each of the four parts of the building. There are always eight people in total. I will explain the deeper meaning of that later. For the time being, Matha and I live in this wing of the building. You will be brought to your own wing, which is exactly the same as the one we have here, but you'll find your own wing completely empty. This might be odd but it may not be satisfactory if someone else furnishes your wing. You must create your own atmosphere and bring your own personality and therefore, you must do the interior designing yourself."

While he is talking, we see again the unmistakable spark of pleasure in Hatma's eyes. They dance. And Matha also looks at us with a smile. What are these two up to?

"It's the practice phase of your education now, after all," Hatma continues. "Therefore, you have to do it yourself."

Oh yes, we understand. It'll be quite a challenge. The whole caboodle must be made by means of our own thought forces, by spiritual building, no doubt about that. We look at each other a little bit disheartened and this makes Hatma burst out in gleeful laughter. In the end, we laugh with him. When Matha places her hands comfortingly on ours, we know we can manage.

35

A Failed Enterprise

A little bit later, Hatma takes us to the side of the building, which we understand will be ours for the moment. We find a large door just like Hatma's because everything looks the same on the outside. We stand in front of the closed door for a while, but there is no Matha or anyone inside to open it for us.

"You do have a key," Matha says almost reproachfully. Ah yes! How could we have forgotten? All of us had received a key in one of the lectures. Before we even can look for the thing, the attention on it has done its job, and the door opens itself. Although Hatma prepared us for the fact that our floor would be free of furnishings, we still fall silent when we see the enormous empty space.

"Before we leave you here," Hatma continues, "I would like to introduce you to your neighbours in the next wing. We'll introduce you to the ones in the last wing later."

The four of us go to the next gallery. Immediately, the door opens and two people welcome us with laughing faces. They are in light blue as we are, and they're wearing the same seal around their neck, confirming they are in the same category as us. But we don't need that clue because the two standing in front of us laugh with so much pleasure when they see our surprised faces. We all laugh. Labino and Labina! It's getting better and better here, and we're now having fun on our new adventure. We even get curious and ask who the last two people in the fourth wing could be. Would we know them as well? But Hatma doesn't seem willing to talk about it and there's already plenty here to occupy our attention. In the meantime, Labino and Labina have asked us to come in and we notice their interior is cosy and tasteful, although completely different from that of Hatma and Matha. The emphasis here is more in the use of plants with single flowers as colourful decorations dotted around, just enough to give an air of sophistication. Labina comes to us with a beautiful plant.

"Here. For your new house, then at least you have something to start with."

It's as if something heavy lifts, and when Matha gives us a beautiful silk carpet, we're on cloud nine and everything looks rosy. Hatma suggests we should go back to our own place, and so we say goodbye to Labino and Labina, while Hatma and Matha also go back to their own wing.

Back at our own house, we put the plant we got from our neighbours on the floor in front of one of the windows looking out on our gallery. Then we look at each other with a big question mark. Although it was easy to fabricate things when Hatma was there to help—and obviously he took the biggest part on his account—we must now do it ourselves. We wonder if we should try a chair first, but we're unsure. Alright then, we have to start somewhere. First, nothing happens. Absolutely nothing. Ha, that's a good start! If we continue like this, we'll never get a fantastic interior. If we're not concentrating enough or we think distracting and negative thoughts, we won't get any result.

Now we must really put in some effort because otherwise we'll never finish. So, to the chair. We concentrate and focus but are still not too tied up in any negative thoughts. It might take a while, but this time we won't give in. Then there is a soft, small mistiness. It clumps together so that it looks like a little cloud. Then the wisps separate and come together again and separate again. Oh my! We almost give up. But we resolve to carry on, otherwise nothing will happen here.

After what seems like forever, there's finally a change in the situation. Here and there we can see something more substantial and after struggling along for a while we see something appear that, with a little bit of goodwill, looks like a leg of a chair and a fragment of cushion. We say this with a pinch of imagination because of course, it's far from perfect. Another leg of the chair evolves and another one and the whole thing is floating and moving through the air to the left, then right as if it's an unorganised bunch of ghosts! What are we going to do with that for heaven's sake? We decide the best idea is to go after it, and see if we can catch it, and perhaps then we can make something out of it. So we run through our empty house, jumping up and down. We must look like a circus! We're so happy that nobody can see us! Ha, ha ha, really?

In the middle of our bumping and jumping and flying around to try to catch the chair, we hear peals of laughter. Labino and Labina are staring through the window crying with hilarity. It must be a ridiculous exhibition to see us there hunting this chair in the air. We also see how comical it must look and we join their laughter. We open the door and let our neighbours in.

"Oh you poor guys!" Labina giggles as she wipes the tears out of her eyes. "We can't help it, but it was such a comical sight to see you jump around after this chair. Why don't you come with us? Then you can take a rest from all the things that you've done and talk about how you can do it better. Everything is going to be alright."

Of course, we want nothing else, so we immediately go outside with them and Labina in the meantime has gone ahead to put easy deck chairs under the green gallery. We sit there and catch our breath and reflect on our failed enterprise, one that cost us a lot of effort. Inside we have many, many questions and it's impossible to keep the most important one quiet.

"How come when we're able to make a whole earth, even a little one, can we not produce a very simple chair?"

36

CLARIFICATION

Now that we have that off our chest, we let them give us an answer.

"Don't get so excited," Labino says. "We'll give you a straight answer. For starters, of course, we know everything about the earth globe you created, and we're thrilled it went well. Still, I have to point out that the beginning of this was in principle already present; you were provided with something already in existence. Remember the cloud you felt attracted to and then, by its own accord, came towards you? In this way, it proved that it already belonged to you. Hatma has already explained why this was, so we don't have to discuss it again.

"After that, Hatma put in the kernel of light along with Matha. Although she wasn't present at the time, she still attached her powers to it. This light is the real living element, and without it, it wouldn't have had a chance to continue existing or grow into a new creation. No human, animal or sentient being in the universe can hope to continue without this kernel of light or soul. You need to have received a soul or a power that is higher than yours to begin.

"Next, you learned to apply the WORD and used it to give the whole thing a material form. It took this particular form with the help of the WORD to bring it into a new creation. I'll give you a better explanation. You would have noticed there were three different phases in this development, and they were all initiated by one pair. The cloud was formulated and brought to existence by Labina and me, the kernel of light by Hatma and Matha, and in the end the materialisation, the substance that really changed it into a sphere, by you. This is a very important point because it shows that it only happens when you have this essential system of polarities: positive–negative, man–woman, plus–minus, attraction–repulsion, or whatever you want to call it. Can you now see why we're educated as couples? It's necessary for the creative process to work for something like this new world. It's a lot more than just a man–woman relationship, which in essence is only the basic principle of reproduction, but it is the forging of two souls, the strength in the power of two."

After this explanation, it's much clearer to us. Labino stops talking, but then Labina continues the discussion.

"So this is the answer to your question related to the world globe. However, it's completely different when it comes to the creation of your own environment, like the things that belong in your home and yourself. So, go back to your house and see for yourself how it works out. What you're creating there is for you alone and so can come from your essence. It's what makes you feel at home, happy and content. When you spend some time in your house, you'll see that everything occurs by itself. It will grow, it will fulfil itself and you won't have to run after the parts of a chair."

"Yes," Labino butts in, "you might find this incomprehensible by comparing it to the process you have on Earth where you go to the shop and buy what you need. It's very easy, convenient, and materialistic, but it has nothing to do with the spirit. But just think about this for a second. Would there be anything on Earth if it wasn't conceptualised by the spirit first? Not even two pieces of wood would be glued together had somebody's mind not thought about it. Only then could it become a reality. Everything, literally everything on Earth, is a product of the spirit, without any exception. And to go a step further, even nature was started with the spirit, only coming to fruition after it was planned out. So in reality, there's no difference to what you're experiencing here. The only difference is that on Earth the materialisation happens in relation to the unique laws on that planet. The material we use here is made out of the spirit. So it's easier because the entire atmosphere is so ripe, so over-saturated with spiritual materials that, in any moment, you can shape it into whatever the spirit of the person wants."

This explanation opens our eyes, and for the first time, we understand so much more, and we're so grateful for Labino and Labina's advice. We continue to chat for a little while, but then we're eager to go back to our own house to see what happens.

We look at it with completely fresh eyes. Observing the empty space, we soon get a clear sense of how we'd like to decorate it, what we'd like to have in it, how to give it its own character and we begin working out all the details. Our enthusiasm grows with each minute. We're so absorbed we don't even notice there's already slowly, very slowly, a manifestation of what we wanted. Instead of focusing on making the objects, the objects have materialised by just thinking about them. We materialise it in our spirit, in our thoughts, and as Labino and Labina predicted, this works. Although at the moment, it's still vague, we know they will solidify and be as good and solid as the items we have seen in the other rooms.

We're so happy. The chairs, the tables, everything is coming together so artfully, and we see the things that we want to use, our musical instruments without which we would definitely not be happy, and soon—but we understand it might take a while—we will see everything around us and if we want to change something, we can do that as well. Then we know we can do this!

37

THE PEOPLE OF THE LIGHT

"Now it's time to visit the last two people of our group. Those who are the closing point of our quadrant," Hatma says to us.

We want that very much and as soon as Hatma, Matha, Labino, Labina, and ourselves are gathered, we move to the fourth door that has been closed until now. We thought it was only us who didn't know but judging by Labino and Labina's facial expression, it's also a mystery for them. With everything going on, we had not spent too much time thinking about it, but now, it gives us a feeling of excitement. Who would we meet here? It has to be someone very special to keep it secret for such a long time.

When we arrive at the fourth door, it opens itself, but there is nobody there to welcome us. A clear light is beaming, and when we step over the threshold, clear rays of light shine over us. We stand there for a moment in suspense. We're filled with anticipation, a feeling of something new occurring, a new birth. The house and the light envelop us so that the suspense becomes an intense force. It becomes stronger and stronger and we feel the force expanding. At that moment, we see two figures in our midst. These figures are different from us. Not in form because they are clearly developed as humans, but their consistency is different. They are made from light and stand in front of us as two radiating light beacons.

We feel nailed to the ground. We can't move nor say a word. This beats all expectations. We also notice that Labino and Labina are in the same surprised state, but then we see a ray of happiness in their eyes, and we also find it in ourselves.

We're over our first surprise and eager to see any further developments. Would Hatma introduce us, or do we have to stand here? We look at him because we still find it a weird moment, and it makes us a little uneasy. We are now familiar with this sense of uneasiness that always comes with the unknown. It's definitely not due to the two light people, because somebody who has so much radiation cannot have a negative influence. This unrest comes only from us, and we mustn't let it take over. Labino and Labina's faces show us they've already controlled their feelings, and therefore, we do our utmost to get control of ourselves.

It seems the two light people were waiting for that because now they point their hands in our direction. A high singing tone goes with it, which we clearly understand means 'welcome'. In response, Matha steps forwards and she sings our introductions to the light couple. We understand this is the language in which these people speak. We also understand that we needn't be uneasy anymore and so we're doing our utmost to stay as calm as possible. What a blessing that Matha is able to function as a translator. It's now obvious to us how Matha represents a bridge, a foot in both worlds. The system is more tightly knitted together than we could have ever imagined.

Matha explains who these two light people are. She is singing both of their names. First the women as she is pointing to her, and we understand this one better than the rest because Matha does it slowly and passionately, and it forms a recognisable pattern. Her name is the three tones sung together combined in a chord. First F-sharp then four tones downwards, C-sharp, then seven higher up, B-sharp. Then Matha sings the man's name, and it's almost the same as the woman's. The same F-sharp and C-sharp but then going up to the next C-sharp, so it swallows the B-sharp of the woman and forms one C-sharp. (We think it interesting that this middle note of the chord comes first). It's also high, so high and yet still so soft. No human voice on earth would ever come close to reaching this sound height but it's beautiful, no question about that. It seems effortless for Matha to sing the pure tones.

When the welcoming ceremony is over, we leave the house of the light people after giving them a silent goodbye. The six of us return to Hatma's house so he can explain this unsettling new experience. When we finally sit down, Hatma speaks.

"It probably was quite a shock to see these two people. They come from a different world. A world where the density of matter is completely different from what we know on Earth, but their mental development is on a much higher level than many other places. These two people came here on the basis of friendship and equality to help us with their wisdom. We're here to complete the task we began when we created the new world. These people will help us make Omega habitable where selected people, those who are ready for higher development can be placed. We'll come together to discuss this on many occasions and this is why the eight of us are gathered in this building. As promised, I'll now explain the symbolic meaning of the figure eight. Eight is the only number that has constant movement in it, never slowing down. The figure eight is a symbol for stability and trustworthiness, both in material and cosmic areas because it's built out of two times four, four material and four cosmic."

38

Music Language

The interior of our house is taking shape and growing. It's probably weird to use the word 'grow', but it's the best way to describe it. The design scheme is becoming denser, and for us it's a constant joy to see its development because it feels uniquely 'us', which you don't always get when you buy an article from a shop. In the meantime, we have received the message that our first introductory meeting will start soon. It's not a meeting in the Earthly sense of the word because then we'd think of sitting around a table and chairs with a chairman, a secretary, and so forth. This is quite different.

In the middle of the courtyard, there are comfortable chairs plonked down at random around the pond.

When we get there, the fish quietly float in the water. They're not playing, so maybe there's some kind of rhythm in their universe as well. It's possible because it seems they also have a kind of consciousness.

All eight of us are seated and we allow the quietness, the peace of being together in this beautiful place, to permeate through us. Oh, we people on Earth are always so absorbed in our hectic life! How we enjoy this moment! As far as we're concerned, we wouldn't mind staying like this forever. But we know it's not possible, and maybe it's good because if not, we'd never be able to look back on how good it was and be grateful for it. With these thoughts in our head, we almost forget why we're actually together here. We're awakened out of our dream when we hear the same soft, high sung tone as before. Now we understand that this tone is the symbol for a welcome and we feel pleased we can distinguish it. We're so grateful we have a strong musical background, otherwise we wouldn't be able to differentiate. Labino and Labina also see it as a natural language, but we're not surprised because the planet where they come from is the one where everything is related to art.

We already know two parts of the new language: the long high tone that is used as a welcome and has a very definite length in time, and then the names of two people. How do we feel about learning this? Well, we're delighted with this knowledge and we can barely control our desire to learn more. We don't have to wait long.

The light man (we have to call him this because we can't call him F-sharp C-sharp C-sharp every time) and the light woman have brought something to show us. It's a kind of egg which is also made from light but looks solid. They place it in front of us so we can observe it and try to figure out what it means. Hatma's lessons were effective because now we have learned to think and feel in symbols and to understand what they mean. So it's not difficult to see the similarity between the egg, which is the basic principle, and the kernel which is the start of all things, the seed of every creation.

As we understand this, the light people sing a tone again. It's a very different tone to the one used to welcome us. We are now sure their language does not contain any words like our language on Earth.

We feel it's the expression of concepts through song. One particular sound or combination of sounds for a concept can mean many things. It seems difficult at first sight (or sound!) but when you think about it, isn't that a simple system? We recognise the similarities between the long tone of the welcome concept and the long tone of the egg, which is like a kernel, the beginning concept. Those tones are on completely different levels, and the tone length is very clear. They all mean the concept of 'beginning' because, in a certain way, being welcomed is also the beginning of something. So we have already worked out that the height of tone, the length of the tone, and yes, also the tone strength play an important role.

They must see on our faces that we have understood the system because they smile, having waited for us to arrive at the conclusion. They continue to explain, and an idea moves through our mind: one cannot go further until the reason for the kernel is completely evaluated and understood and 'planted' in the big picture. With intense concentration we look at them. It's so kind of them to put the concepts so graphically because they could have sung something for us, and we wouldn't have understood one syllable. Hatma turns to us.

"The tone for the concept 'germ cell'," he explains, "is the longest that's ever used because when the egg is being created, it needs a long period of thought; a period of development."

We need this explanation. It was obviously not in our unspoken mental exercise.

"Thank you, Hatma," we say.

In front of our eyes the egg opens. The light people have two identical parts in their hands. We can see what's in there, and although we don't understand what it means, we see that one half consists of pure radiating light and the other half an opaquer consistency. We can't say that it's light and therefore dark because that is definitely not the case. It would probably be more correct to say that the second half of the egg is like a shadow of the first and that's the reason there's this kind of timbre, the colour of the sound when it's made into a tone. So that means that our field of knowledge is now larger, and we have different nuances which all can have their own concept. They don't give us any more tones. We have to satisfy ourselves with the germ cell concept and the knowledge that there could be many combinations.

39

MEETING

"It's not our intention to give you an education of a new language," Hatma says when we meet him later on. "It's given you an impression of the principles used, though. To go deeper, you need a more comprehensive musical knowledge of that which is available on Earth. Instead, we must put one hundred percent of our attention to what we are primarily here for. Namely, to discuss the subject of the eventual use and location of our new world ball. I see that you're wondering why I used the word 'eventual' and maybe you thought that this was by accident or a pun. Remember, though, it will make you understand things much faster."

After some time we're back, the eight of us gathered on the grass around the pond. This time, we're positioned so that each couple is sitting on the same side as their rooms. We understand this has a deeper meaning; that each person talks from their own point of view, from their own terrain. In this way, we have less friction, and we won't waste time. Hatma smiles when he catches our line of thought, and he nods at us in an affirmative way.

The fish in the pond swim quietly and instead of being a distraction, they make us feel peaceful and calm. The clear water also feeds a sense of serenity, and we all feel as good as can be. Don't get the impression that we must yell at each other over the pond from all sides to make ourselves heard. No, the atmosphere here is so pure, we're convinced that even the softest-spoken word will be clearly audible. Again Hatma looks at us, but now he has a mysterious smile on his face. We lounge on our comfortable deck chairs and it's lovely. Deep inner peace intensifies by the minute. There is no sound or movement from anyone. Everything is so quiet, so good. We're not thinking or even amazed over the fact that there's no official start to the meeting. We just let it happen as it comes.

Then finally, we hear the long tone. The tone of welcome from the people of the light. We think we hear it, even so, it wasn't exactly there. What was it then? This tone has woken us up from our thoughts. It was absolutely real, but our ears didn't pick it up. We see the others heard it too by the expression of concentration on their faces. If we didn't hear it through our ears, then it has to have come from inside us. Ah! There it is again.

This time it's not a tone but a short concept, namely: who wants to bring the first suggestion to the table? For a moment, we imagine 'to the table' should be 'to the pond'! First, we should not let our thoughts meander but concentrate, and second, the concept is not like a sentence that has been put forward.

Soon there's another tone: that we must know the end goal in order to find the beginning. So first we must agree on what the final result should be. That is the goal we should work towards to make our world ball a perfect destination. We must discuss what themes it will have because every planet, every world, is based on something special. We must follow this line of discussion to reach the desired outcome.

So this is the way our meetings go. There is no obstruction in speaking different languages. We can all understand each other and exchange thoughts; thoughts that will come out of our deepest selves but are not brought forward through spoken words or even sounds. The beauty of this is only our pure inner selves are expressed without fear of any misinterpretation that words and even sounds can have.

Meetings usually begin with each person bringing his vision or agenda to the table and before long, everyone's ideas and opinions are clashing left, right and centre. But not here. We notice there's quite a unique system in practice. Here they start with the germ cell, which doesn't mean the germ cell of the beginning of a new world ball because that's already there, but the germ cell of the subject that's at hand. One tries to find the smallest, first point in which all of us agree in every aspect, where all the extraneous details are stripped away and only the essence is left. Sometimes only a small part of the suggestions made are used, and that's only when everyone agrees one hundred percent it's the best idea for the final concept.

It's an extraordinary experience. The main concept doesn't proceed until everybody is in agreement. If not, we go back to the lowest point of agreement and only then continue by adding or discussing according to the same principle. In this way, there's never anything introduced where we are not all in agreement.

We ourselves make a small contribution and although the insight and the wisdom of the others are at a much higher level than ours, once in a while they do add part of our suggestions. When that happens, we feel ecstatic!

The entire meeting is used to discuss only the subject that was put forward and it's completely irrelevant how much time we take. We're so engaged in this task that we don't even notice the time. The main thing is to find what's necessary for the maturation of our young world.

We won't go into detail here about the plans for the world. The people of Earth could strive to think at a higher level and try to quell their curiosity by trust— trusting that the end will be just as it should be, good and pure.

40

FROM POINT TO POINT

It has taken a long time to go over this matter, a time of hard inner work. It was never an easy task, but it was breathtaking what we achieved in such a short time. When we finally determined the final purpose, everything moved a little bit easier. The timings needed for the complete development of the new world needed to be fixed on certain points. Then the phases in between the points needed to be filled. But there was more freedom here so that it had a chance to develop, to grow and to become itself. It was important to work to each point instinctively but at the same time, keep in mind the whole picture.

The sphere also manifested itself in surprising ways, allowing us to draw impulses from it. There was a danger that this could get out of hand, but the regular fixed points kept everything together. These elements were an intrinsic, untouchable part of the organism of this world and therefore, it determined its own being.

At the end, the entire plan was documented on a specially made scroll, which was archived. We, all eight of us, put our seal (which we received for such events!) underneath, and the fate of our new world was indeed sealed. What a beautiful feeling it gives us to know that the whole scheme and every little detail has a good, pure nucleus, a kernel. There are no weak or trivial concepts but strong, stimulating, advancing realities.

The full glory of this creation sinks in; how every detail was considered with attention and precision. The smallest kernel of impurity or negligence would potentially grow into an indescribable disaster!

Another important matter is the protecting ring, which will need to be constructed once 'Omega' is fully grown. This is the last phase which will be conducted by the two light people. Our planet will also get a more personal character along with the ring, an influence which will be combined with ours, and this will form the basic principle of this new world.

A new type of human race will live here, selected from other races, spiritually ready to receive the new element of the light. In this way, they will follow an evolutionary path that will allow them to exist in a way which is over the horizon of our current earthly human understanding. To the other six of our group, it may already be known. We suspect so from our meetings. It's fantastic, we think, that Hatma has involved us. Who do we owe that to? We don't think about it too much otherwise we might get an inferiority complex! There will indeed be future challenges, so it's better to simply surrender ourselves to what may be and do our best. The only thing left is for us to do our best.

41

The End and a New Beginning

Humanly speaking, we would now be at the end and would expect a climax, but here we have different norms. No finale with a fanfare, no official meeting with speeches. Quietly, as if it's a daily event, we say goodbye to all those with whom we've worked for such a long time. We know it won't be adieu forever.

Hatma goes with us on our way back, and we soon notice that it's not completely over because we are taken to the place where we met Hatma for the first time: the open building with the dome, the wide view, the silent peace. What a long way we've travelled between now and then and how much richer we are because of it.

We're seated on the floor again just like in the beginning, and we let our eyes scan the golden scenery, but we don't speak. Hatma is also quiet. There is nothing more to say. We exist like always, but we now live deep in ourselves. What more can we ask than to sit here untroubled by any influence from the outside? We have learned so much. We understand one step follows the other. That there is always a solution for every difficulty. That there is a kernel in all things, and there is a final goal that everything works towards.

We also learned that those who have a task to do must follow through, whatever the problems may be. And therefore we mustn't forget that we must continue—that we can do nothing but continue.

Then, when all these thoughts are in us and the only element within is deep silence, something breaks this peace. It's a voice so clear and a light so pure. We listen with deep attention, as does Hatma, who has an expression of happiness on his face.

"The seven seals will be taken away,

The seven books will be opened,

The seven heavens will open."

Then we hear nothing, just silence and peace. And slowly we see Hatma fade away. His figure becomes transparent and then he disappears, leaving us here without a single word. But within us, there is singing, as if all the voices that ever existed have come together. As a radiant chorus the sound builds up to a unity that's unbreakable and is the foundation for everything in front of us. Thank you dear God, for the past, for the now, and for the future.

Afterword

The acceleration of technological progress has brought our life's relationships, both personal and professional, mostly to a virtual level. This makes us constantly connected, but without being truly connected to ourselves. Often, we are not able to regain mastery of our life, to manage its rhythms and appreciate the important things we should be, could be doing. The positive, hope-filled expectations about our lives and our futures that prevailed but a decade or two ago have vanished. We are blundering forward, without a sense of purpose and without a vision of who we are and what we are here for. We have lost touch with nature and the universe, lost the sense of community and oneness that is the foundation of health and well-being. We no longer know where to turn, or whom and what to trust. We are not even sure that we can survive the mounting crises that appear on the horizon (ninety seconds before twelve). We appear to have lost our way.

"The Book of HATMA" is not a fairy-tale, it is reality and, in today's quantum world as postulated by David Bohm, we can understand that.

My wife, Marie Louise, died on the 10th of November 2022. I offer you part of my eulogy to explain:

"And then we have the issue of the cat.

Bear with me, this part is the fault of my mate Alan and our conversations about quantum physics and my friend Rob and his music, impregnating our lives.

Nobel prize winner Niels Bohr stated in 1955 that 'Everything we call real, is made of things that cannot be regarded as real.'

And US astrophysicist Hakeem Oluseyi, more recently in 2021 agreed that 'Matter, mass, none of it exists. It's all an illusion.'

If you have heard of any quantum scientist from the 1930s, it is likely to be the Austrian physicist

Erwin Schrödinger. Or, more likely, his cat. The cat of course never existed and neither did any experiment involving animals of any kind. Schrödinger's now famous 1935 thought exercise was constructed to poke holes in the new quantum theory. In the fanciful feline experiment, you place a cat in a box with radioactive stuff, which, as it decays releases a poison that snuffs out Fluffy. The principle of superposition suggests that two states now arise: in one the radioactive substance starts to decay and in the other, it doesn't. Both states are in play, meaning that the cat in the box is neither alive nor dead but both at the same time. When we open the box, the two states collapse into one: Fluffy is either with us or snoozing.

So, what is this quantum physics? Quantum physics is simply the description of how small things, like atoms, behave, and they behave in a bizarre way. Every time they interact with something, they are in a specific position, but when they are not interacting with anything, they spread out in space, so they can, for instance, pass through two different spaces at once. In other words, the cause-and-effect notions we have of basic physics fall apart as we go down to the micro level. Space is granular, time does not exist, and things are nowhere. Reality is not as it appears to us.

But more on that later. First, let's back up a little and head back to where it all began.

The concept of the atom had been kicking around since the Milesians of 450 BC; a group of very science-y, free-thinking philosophers who asked lots of questions about the world and what it's made of, including the stuff that makes us. It was Democritus who nailed it when he took an apple and suggested that if he cut it up into smaller and smaller pieces, eventually he would get to a tiny indivisible piece that, along with others, form and reform to create everything around us, from water drops to mountain tops. He called it atmos, or 'uncuttable'. Atomic theory was born!

Then Aristotle pooh-poohed the idea, asserting that the world is instead made of 4 elements: earth, air, fire and water. Aristotle was famous and influential, so the Democritus camp changed its tune and atmos was quickly forgotten. After a long, dull Middle Ages (where science came up against fundamental

Christianity and lost), things picked up again. Almost biblically, Democritus' apple is at the core of another turning point in science when it fell beside—not on—the head of 23-year-old Isaac Newton while he was relaxing in the orchard of his family farm. Newton was a young and brilliant loner, who mathematised everything around him, leading to breakthroughs in optics, colour and the nature of light. Twenty years on from the apple incident, and after being prodded by fellow astronomer Edmond Haley about the nature of comets, Newton dug deep into gravity. He threw himself into the mathematics of the whole universe. In 1686, he presented his 3 laws of motion, which helped explain the modern concept of science with his devotion to observation and results-based testing. He changed entirely how we view the world and, at a macro level, we still live in a Newtonian world today. Although paradigm-shifting, Newton knew his laws didn't really explain the world. Yes, the Moon is attracted to the Earth, but how? What physically draws the two together? Or us to the ground? Newton couldn't say. In 1852, Michael Faraday who studied electricity and magnetism and the brilliant young mathematician James Maxwell came up with the idea of 'field' that is spread throughout space as the uniting force which physically holds everything together. The Maxwell-Faraday fields replaced Newton's empty space, and we still use those equations today to describe all electrical and magnetic phenomena, from building an aerial to understanding the sun.

Then came Albert. In 1905, in what became known as his Annus Mirabilis (miracle year), a brilliant German patent clerk named Albert Einstein submitted 4 papers to a scientific journal, all of which were game changers. The first paper explained the photoelectric effect and earned him a Nobel prize, while the third paper outlines his theory of relativity, which showed that time was relative rather than absolute.

There was no longer empty space with stuff in it, but fields like an ocean that holds everything together. Think of space as a large sheet stretched out in all directions, constantly undulating and changing, with the planets plonked in it like billiard balls. Space warps around large bodies such as planets, bending time and light with it, and creates black holes that absorb all in their grasp.

While all of this sounded like crazy fiction at the time, experiment after experiment has shown it to be true. Black holes, once fanciful, are now seen in abundance, and light has proven to bend as it travels around the sun. Einstein's General Theory of Relativity has been called the greatest achievement of mankind. Albert's next step was subatomic. Quantum.

German physicist Max Planck discovered in 1901 that light is emitted in discrete, measurable packets. He called these packets of energy "quanta" (from the Latin quantus, how much) and was able to come up with a number: a value for one packet of energy, which we now call a photon. So, one photon of light has one quantum of energy. Light is a stream of photons, which are always in motion and in a vacuum and travel at a constant speed: the speed of light. Quantum physics suggests that the world, not just light but everything, is quantised—that is, made of discrete packets, assuming even gravity.

Keeping up? Let's quickly go back to the 19th century when in 1803 the chemist John Dalton picked up on Democritus' atoms and applied real science to what was only philosophical musing before. Studying gases, he found that atoms, in fact, were actual things: solid balls that could neither be created nor destroyed. And eighty years later, JJ Thompson noted electrical charges and declared that something was inside each atom: electrons, which he suggested were like plums in a pudding. It was called the plum pudding theory. New Zealander Ernest Rutherford then suggested electrons were not static but whizzed about and finally Niels Bohr re-imagined the model again. Electrons, he stated, orbited the nucleus on their own distinct paths, and the burst of energy that we know as atomic power was the effect of one electron leaping from a higher frequency orbit to a lower one: the quantum leap. But, in 1932, one of Niels' assistants, Werner Heisenberg got his Nobel prize for noting that there was no such thing as an electron in an orbit. Strange things happened inside an atom. Nothing was behaving according to the rules of nature. Sub-atomic particles could be nowhere and everywhere at once. And observing them seemed to change their behaviour. Quantum physics shook the world and has alarmed scientists ever since. While the maths has proved infallible at every turn—GPS, USB drives and MRI machines are tangible results—argument continues to rage about what actually happens.

Just to mention two oddities:

1. Entanglement

The strangest phenomenon is entanglement which lies at the heart of quantum physics. A subatomic particle here and one at the other end of the universe (or in the next room) act as one and become 'entangled'. If one turns blue, so does the other. The connection is instant, faster than the speed of light (or even thought?). No physical phenomenon that we know explains this connection. Einstein famously called it "spooky action at a distance". We can know everything that can be known about two single separate particles and yet there are still other properties of the two together.

2. Superposition

Then there is superposition, the idea that a particle can be in two states at once…

So, where are we now? What's really happening? There are at the moment three current theories:

1. Many-worlds interpretation.

If you stub your toe there is a version of you that didn't, and a version of you that completely fell over. First suggested by US physicist Hugh Everett in the late 1950's MWI envisions our physical universe as just one of infinite parallel worlds that continually spin off from each other. While they all exist in the same space and time, they are completely whole and independent of our reality. Hollywood and sci-fi authors love this concept.

2. Hidden-variables theory

On the surface it would seem that the quantum world doesn't follow the rules of nature: that is cause and effect. Instead, it embraces probability and spooky invisible communication. But the Hidden-variables theory suggests it is our knowledge of physical reality that is lacking. The truth is out there, it just needs to be discovered.

3. Relational theory

Nothing exists until it bumps into something else, this theory has gained traction. Facts are simply interactions between any two physical systems and are relative to these systems: if a tree falls in a forest and no one is there to hear it, does it make a sound? Well, if it has nothing to bounce off, to interpret it and respond, to hear it...then perhaps not...

There is a pragmatic scientific mantra that says, 'shut up and compute': even if we don't know how the universe works, we sure know how to harness it. Quantum physics powers our modern world from light switches to microchips and is marching us towards quantum computers. More than 2500 years ago, apple-wielding Democritus and his fellow Milesians questioned everything. Physics and philosophy are ultimately inseparable: you can't look deeply into the heart of what makes us and not ask how. Or why.

'The most beautiful thing we can experience,' Albert Einstein wrote in his 1930 philosophical essay, What I Believe[1], 'is the mysterious. It is the source of true art and emotion.'

And that's why I believe that when I was holding my wife's hand and saw her last, very last breath leaving her body, like the cat; looking away she, in her essence, would be there, in the beautiful garden surrounded with this little stone wall[2]—waiting till the time I'd come. Knowing what I have learnt about quantum physics and reading the extraordinary words gives me great peace. I like to see Marie-Louise in the peaceful, love-filled and expanding world described in this book.

In 2001 a Dutch cardiologist, Dr Pim van Lommel, published in the prestigious medical journal The Lancet, a first; the largest study done in survivors of cardiac arrest and their near-death experiences (NDE). It was a prospective study including 344 consecutive cardiac patients who were successfully resuscitated after cardiac arrest in ten Dutch hospitals. They compared demographic, medical, pharmacological, and psychological data between patients who reported NDE (18%) and patients who did not (controls) after resuscitation. In a longitudinal study of life changes after NDE, they compared the groups 2 and 8 years later.[3] He poses some interesting questions whilst discussing the astounding results: "How could a clear consciousness outside one's body be experienced at the moment that the brain no longer functions during a period of clinical death with a flat EEG?" Dr van Lommel then concludes: "There is no life after death, but there is continuation of consciousness."

And so, this story, written in 1955, comes to life. It might give us hope that we can still find again our inner self. Ervin Laszlo, in his book The Wisdom Principles[4] states:

"There is widespread fallacy today in the world: if we do not perceive something, and if we cannot account for it in relation to the perceivable world, we say it doesn't exist. This is a fallacy because the real world is far wider and deeper than we have thought. There could be entire dimensions of reality we do not perceive, and yet are real. What we have known as the 'spiritual world' could be such a dimension."

So, we move on, my friend will try to teach me jazz piano and I give you one thought to ponder:

That which gives meaning and purpose in life may change over the years. After all, very few things ever stay the same. The water in a closed pool only stagnates over time. It is the flowing water, ever on its winding path, that stays fresh.

1.

   https://opensiddur.org/wp-content/uploads/2019/02/What-I-Believe-Albert-Einstein-1930.pdf

2. This garden is described in the The Book of Godfried that was written after Hatma. Het boek Godfried. Roma Hijneman 1975, Uitgeverij de Fontein bv, De Bilt, isbn 90 261 3021 x (in Dutch)

3. Near-Death experience in survivors of cardiac arrest: a prospective study in the Netherlands. P van Lommel et al, Lancet 2002 April 6;359(9313):1254

4. The Wisdom Principles. Ervin Laszlo,2021, St Martin's Publishing Group, isbn 9781250797216

Also By Atem

Return Trip to Moses

Dhawana

(Above published by Red Feather Publishing)

The Book of Eron

The Book of Godfried. 1975, Uitgeverij de Fontein
bv, De Bilt ISBN 90 261 3021 x (in Dutch)

Het boek van de Eeuwigheid. 1996, Uitgeverij Kairos,
Soest, ISBN 90 70338 467/cip (in Dutch)

Mijn Hemel, wat nu? 1975, Uitgeverij de Fontein bv,
De Bilt, ISBN 90 261 3017 1 (in Dutch)